Mrs. Hungerford

A Born Coquette

Vol. III

Mrs. Hungerford

A Born Coquette
Vol. III

ISBN/EAN: 9783337053109

Printed in Europe, USA, Canada, Australia, Japan

Cover: Foto ©Andreas Hilbeck / pixelio.de

More available books at **www.hansebooks.com**

QUETTE

IN THREE VOLUMES
VOL. III.

LONDON
SPENCER BLACKETT
35, ST. BRIDE STREET, LUDGATE CIRCUS, E.C.
1890

A BORN COQUETTE.

CHAPTER I.

'Il y en a toujours l'un qui baise,
Et l'autre qui tend la joue.'

'He gives his love, his life, his hopes ;
She gives her smiles—a few.'

*   *   *   *   *

'Is that you? Come in here for one moment.
Such good news!' cries Nan, rushing into the
corridor as she hears her husband's step pass the
door, and dragging him into her dressing-room,
where sits Bartle in all the glory of a new and per-
fectly-built suit of evening clothes—the result of his
brother-in-law's last kindly 'tip.'

'He has passed !' goes on Nan, still with her hand

on Hume's arm, and staring into his face to see if his satisfaction is equal to her own—to note the glad triumph that she expects to see there. Providentially she does see it. 'He heard only this morning, and hurried home. Isn't it glorious news? He has passed for the Civil Service. Now, didn't I always say it? Isn't he clever?'

'He makes one proud of him,' says Hume with a smile at Bartle, who is blushing beneath this heavy weight of praise.

He is quite aware that his wife's delight and excitement has led her into this sudden friendliness. To declare her joyful news is a necessity to her ; and if he had not been present at the moment another would have served her purpose just as well. He is not dead to all these facts : yet, for all that, a thrill of happiness warms his veins, as he feels her hand upon his arm. She could not really hate him, and then ask him to participate in her exultation.

'I do most heartily congratulate you,' he says, going up to the handsome lad and warmly shaking his hand.

'It isn't anything so very much out of the way,

really,' says Bartle shamefacedly. ' So many other
fellows have done even better. And,' with a glance
of gratitude, ' other fellows haven't had the advantage
of such a first-class coach as I had — thanks to
you.'

'Yes, yes, you have been good about this,' says
Nan, who has gone back to the dressing-table, and
is busy putting on her bracelets. It is the night of
her ball, and in her white gown of lace and satin
she looks likes a dream of one fair woman, at all
events. Even as she looks back over her shoulder
to say this, a little cry escapes her.

' Oh, there's a pin sticking into my shoulder somewhere, and I've sent Susan away ! There, there it is
again,' making a little miserable moan, ' and I can't
get at it, it is so far back. Could either of you help
me, I wonder ?'

' I'll try,' says Hume promptly, yet with a certain
diffidence.

' Well, it is just there,' shrugging up her shoulder,
to give assistance to her words. ' Ah, how it hurts
me !'

Hume bends over her assiduously, and with gentle

fingers searches for the offending pin. Her lovely
neck, fair and boneless as a little child's, is very near
him. The diamond string surrounding it rises and
falls with every breath. Such a perfect neck! He
would have given anything to be able to stoop and
kiss it; yet not for anything would he have done it.
He is a long time accomplishing his task—not of set
purpose—but because of natural awkwardness, and as
natural a desire to be as little awkward as possible.
His untaught fingers, taking an unlucky turn, drive
the implement of torture once more into the tender
flesh.

'Ah!' cries Nan with a little, soft, delicate shriek.
'Oh dear! Why did I ask you? What a useless
person you are!'

'I have it, however,' says Hume, emerging
crimson and breathless from behind her shoulder,
and holding up the wicked pin to public condemnation.

'Oh, what a blessing!' says Mrs. Hume thankfully.
She still shrugs her shoulder, however, as if the smart
has not yet quite departed.

'Does it hurt you still?' asks Hume anxiously.

'Let me see,' he draws down the laces that border her gown, and gazes attentively at the mark. It is so small, that it takes some time to find it. 'It is nothing,' says he, with as much relief in his tone as if she had suddenly been declared out of danger of death. 'You could hardly see it.'

'Well, it was horrid while it lasted, at all events,' says Nan, pulling on her gloves. She moves to a mirror and surveys her perfect self with very frank satisfaction.

'How do I look?' says she, glancing back at the others with a half coquettish, half abashed smile.

'Not so bad as you might,' says Bartle pleasantly.

'Pouf!' says she, making a little contemptuous gesture towards him, and turning at once to Hume. 'Well?' says she, in a rather challenging tone. Bartle's success has put her in the highest spirits. As she speaks her eyes meet Hume's, and there is something in his that for the moment suppresses all feelings within her, save one—a strange, bewildering shyness. A moment only, then the thraldom ends.

'There is no word,' says Hume in a low voice, and pauses.

She has had time to recover.

'Come, come on, both of you,' says she, a little confusedly still. 'I expect I'm late as it is. By-the-bye, do either of you know whether Freddy Croker has arrived yet? He was to have been here by the afternoon train, but I suppose he managed to miss that. Barristers in practice give themselves such airs.'

'If so, he can't be here till eleven,' says Bartle. 'Last train.'

It is indeed twelve o'clock before Croker arrives. Coming down from the apartment given to him at Hume, he traverses the halls, and going towards the reception rooms upon his left, happens to pass through a tiny ante-chamber smothered in flowers. It has been evidently fitted up to meet the requirements of engaged, or otherwise promising couples, and is but dimly lit. It is plainly a place set apart—a sitting-out arrangement—sufficiently remote and cosy to suit the taste of any true lover.

Mr. Croker entering it, with a view to passing through its further door on his way to the drawing-rooms, makes a little involuntary halt on the threshold. Upon a lounge of maize-coloured satin, beneath the shadow of two overhanging palms, sits Penelope with Boyle Ffrench beside her.

Unfortunately Penelope does not see him, and unfortunately too Boyle, who is in one of his lachrymose moods, is pouring out to her his troubles in such eloquently rounded periods, that perforce she is impressed by him. She is leaning forward, her gentle face full of tender sympathy, her whole bearing suggestive of no ordinary amount of interest in what is being said. Boyle, too, is looking impassioned—through his woes, not through his affections—a subtle difference not to be understood by the casual observer.

Croker, after a lengthened gaze at the abstracted couple, retraces his footsteps, and makes his way to his hostess by another route.

*   *   *   *   *

The night verges towards morning, though so dull is the wintry dark that no one takes heed of it. Stars still burn coldly in the sky, and a brilliant moon enlivens the world below. The ball, so far as a superficial looker-on could judge, has been a brilliant success—to one or two, perhaps, it has been a heart-break.

On his first arrival, Nan, encountering Croker, had been shocked by his appearance. He was haggard, worn, dispirited beyond belief.

'Why, Freddy, how is it with you?' cries she, holding the hand he has given her. The suspicion of treachery towards Penelope had lost ground at once on that first glance. 'You look so terribly pale. So unstrung—so——'

'It seems so absurd,' says he, with a smile. 'But the fact is that I expect I have overworked myself. An evil easily remedied. Don't mind me; don't waste your time thinking about me, I shall do very well.'

'You have seen Penelope?'

'Not yet,' telling his lie calmly. 'Later on, no doubt, she will be good enough to give a dance to an old friend.'

Nan, not altogether contented with his manner, was compelled to let him go by her then, and give her attention—a careless one—to some new guests.

As for her, she is undoubtedly the most beautiful

woman present. Every man in the room, and even a few women, acknowledge that fact. Her brilliant spirits, laughing eyes, the wonderful gaiety, irrepressible, yet delicately subdued, that distinguishes every word and glance, are all a separate beauty in themselves. Though excellent as a hostess, she manages entirely to enjoy herself. Dancing incessantly, yet ever with an eye upon the sighing wallflowers.

It is, of course, impossible that so charming a figure can escape general observation and close scrutiny. After awhile it is remarked that Mrs. Hume is dancing a great deal with Captain Ffrench. 'There was a little *affaire* there before her marriage, eh ?' To give Ffrench full justice, he is as perfect a waltzer as one can find out of Austria, and it is, perhaps, natural that Nan—who is grace itself, and light as feather-down, when good music moves the air—should be glad to have him as a partner. As a matter of fact she thinks no more of him than as a friend of old standing, with whom lies the incomparable quality that permits her to make herself at home with him. So careful has Ffrench proved that no suspicion of the passion that still warms his breast for her has reached her.

He has been particular, too, to be most attentive to Penelope. He has noted part of the public gossip, which has declared him in love with her, he has noted too the other side of the question which has given him to Nan. This last he has agreed within himself to ignore and to defeat by a persistent attention to her sister. To do him justice again, there is no cruelty contained in this decision on his part. No man is surer that Penelope cares nothing for him than he is. Penelope he cannot injure—but Nan——

Revenge, as well as passion, stirs him. Perhaps the former is the stronger feeling. She had led him on, deliberately as it seems to him ; and now—that she does not love Hume is patent to an interested observer. Therefore, according to Captain Ffrench, she married him for his money. Such nervous dread, such fear of public contumely as moved foolish Nan to accept the fate that seemed the only one left her, could not be understood by such a man as Ffrench. The two, therefore, she and Hume, had conspired against his happiness. If he could only feel himself equal with them! He pants for an opportunity to stand before Hume and cry 'quits' with him, though death itself might be his next portion; and as for Nan—well, his thoughts take no shape there in his revenge. His nature has been warped, stunted, yet honestly he loves Nan, and now that she is lost to him, feels anguish at the recollection that there might have been a time when he would not have considered the world well lost for her.

To-night at all events he is happy beyond all hope. Circumstances have been exceptionally kind to him. Every dance he has not danced with Penelope he has danced with Nan.

CHAPTER II.

'The moral doorstep
Cautiously you never o'erstep
When your victims you ensnare,
Lead them on with hopes, deceive them,
Then turn coldly round, and leave them,
Beauty Clare.'

*   *   *   *   *

IT is an hour or two after supper. If it were summer-time the dawn would have broken long ere this, and a lovely cold blue light would be fighting with the lamps in halls and corridors and rooms. Nan, crossing the gallery—still a-gleam with coloured lights—stops half-way as she sees Penelope approaching her. Penelope is alone, and Nan with a little gracious word or two dismisses her partner.

'What a blessing to meet you, Pen,' says she, catching her sister and attempting to draw her on to an ottoman beside her. 'I'm as tired as a frivolous butterfly ought to be—for her sins.'

Penelope resists her a little. This is so strange a thing that Nan directs a more searching gaze at her.

'You are looking lovely,' she says thoughtfully; 'your gown suits you à *merveille*, and yet—what is it, Pen ?'

'Sins,' says Penelope, as thoughtfully. 'Your sins are small ; but your indiscretions——'

'Oh, goodness ! What have I done now ?' exclaims Mrs. Hume, sinking back on the cushions, with an accent of despair. 'Get it out, Pen,' implores she, after a few minutes spent not altogether unpleasantly in a state of repose. 'You'll feel so much better when you've said it ; and so shall I.'

'It is so little, yet so much,' says Penelope, who is plainly greatly distressed. 'I wanted to see you long before this, but it was so difficult to say a word privately. Nanny, darling, why are you dancing so much with Boyle ?'

'Eh ?' cries Nan, jumping out of her pillows with quite an alarming haste. 'So that's it, is it ? And please you, madam, why should I not dance with him ?'

'I leave that to yourself,' says Penelope coldly.

It is the first time that cold words from Penelope addressed to Nan have been heard. The latter's heart shrinks within her. Penny, to speak to her like that!

'One must dance with somebody, if only to keep up a good example,' she says, knowing that Penelope is thinking of that old one-sided love story, and firmly believing it is for Boyle's sake she is speaking.

'There are other people. And as for a good example! Is it good? Give it up, Nan ; it will not serve you or anyone.'

This is positive harshness from the gentle Penelope. Is it, can it be possible that she is jealous of Boyle's attentions to her—Nan? Oh no, that would be horrible! He is so far beneath Penelope in every way!

'Give up what?' asks she.

'Give up this ridiculous flirtation with Boyle. Why should you waste your time with him ?'

'Why should you ?' returns Nan, apparently with

amusement; in reality with some anxiety. 'You have danced with him half the night.'

'To prevent you from dancing with him all the night,' says Penelope, in a low tone, but forcibly.

'Penelope!' says Nan, springing to her feet.

'Yes, I know,' says Penelope, 'you will probably never forgive me; yet in spite of that thought—a thought that makes life worthless—I will speak. Has it never occurred to you that George must suffer when people's tongues wag about his wife? No, no, Nan, listen to me. I shall not speak again, be sure of that. I shall say all now. You are angry because I take George's part, but it is for your sake I take it. This ignoble trifling with your happiness is surely unworthy of you.'

It seems to Nan that Penelope has grown taller, statelier, colder. She is the gentlest creature alive. But even such sweet spirits can at times be roused by grief, by fear for those they love; Penelope's fear is for Nan, and it carries her out of herself. 'Heat sugar,' says Victor Hugo, 'and it will boil.'

'I have no happiness,' says Nan a little slowly, a

little coldly ; 'and as to trifling, why should you use that word to me, Penelope ?'

'Oh, Nan, if I have done wrong to speak,' cries Penelope, her eyes filling with tears—tears in her trembling voice.

'Tut ! Don't make a mountain out of such a mole-hill,' says Nan lightly, but still very coldly. Then, seeing Penelope's saddened face, she relents. 'So after all you are not enjoying yourself,' she says, with a little rush of remorse.

'You must not think that. It is a delightful even-ing—only——'

'Now, now, now ; not another word,' cries Nan, with a gay yet meaning smile, as somebody parts the far curtains and comes towards them.

It is Boyle.

'Our dance, I think, Penelope,' says he.

Penelope, rising with alacrity, carries him off, leaving Nan staring after her.

What does her alacrity mean ? Surely, surely, she could not have been in earnest when she seemed to accuse her of a serious flirtation with Boyle. That is beyond belief; but almost as far out of reach of reality appears the thought that Penelope and jealousy can be in any way connected.

And yet, can it be possible that she really likes the gloomy youth? He has certainly been very attentive to her of late, but this hardly seems a sufficient reason for believing her foolish enough to lose her heart to him. He would be a wretched match for her. Julia's promises of leaving him money are not to be depended on—besides which, Julia is the sort of person who would live for spite. It would be a case of 'live horse till you get grass;' and even giving him all the money in the world, would not his temper alone make him ineligible?

No; Penelope ought to marry Fred Croker, or, in default of him, Lord Cashelmore.

Then suddenly her thoughts veer round, and it occurs to her that all this is rather hard upon Boyle. Suppose he has fallen in love with Penelope; everything seems to point that way. He dances attendance upon her from morning till night, making himself specially conspicuous in his devotion on every public occasion. It is a trifle absurd of him, of course, to go about falling in love with one sister after another, but

after all perhaps he can't help it. Here a sudden
fancy comes to her, and she gives way to a smothered
laugh, though there is no one really to hear her.
When Penelope marries Freddy will he fall in love
with Gladys; and if that little trifler fails him, will he
still come up smiling to take his 'No' from Nolly?

Poor old Boyle! it is a shame to laugh at him like
this. If he has set his affections on Penny, and she
will none of him, that will mean his twice being disappointed. She feels positively grieved for him, as
she gets to this point, and decides, unconsciously, on
being better to him than ever, if only to make it up
to him a bit.

What on earth had Penny meant by speaking to
her with such severity about her dancing so much
with him? That was puzzling. The first half-con-
scious thought recurs to her; and, having now gained
force, brings a hot flush to her cheeks. No, it was
not jealousy, it was censure. Censure, pure and
simple, and from Penelope! Good heavens! What
next? First her husband, then her sister; and all
about what?—nothing. How stupid it all is; stupider
of Penelope, however, than of the others. She ought

to know how unlikely it is she should encourage Boyle now, when all her life she has been so indifferent to him.

At this point her unpleasant reverie is interrupted by the entrance of a young man in hussar uniform, with a huge body, and a baby face.

'Found you at last, Mrs. Hume,' says he in a tone of triumph. 'You've done me out of half my dance, however.'

'You see there really is no peace for the wicked,' says Nan, rising with a little yawn.

'Oh, if you are tired—if you would rather sit here and rest——' begins he heroically, though with disappointment not to be disguised.

To be seen dancing with the beautiful Mrs. Hume is a decided feather in one's shako.

'Tired!' cries Nan gaily, seeing the flattening depression that makes his infantile features almost comic. 'Who ever saw me tired? No, it was merely the laziness of a moment. In truth I am as glad to see you as though you were a flower o' May; one's own company is but a poor thing at the best of times.'

'If you can say that it's a bad look-out for the rest

of us,' says the big boy, with clumsy gallantry, but so
honestly that Nan's heart warms to him, and she gives
him an excellent *quart d'heure*, and sends him away
at the expiration of his time in a lovely mood with
himself and all the world.

She is kinder to others than they are to her, it
seems. But it gives her heart pleasure to make her
guests happy, and later on hardly the most faded
flower amongst them goes home from this her
hostess's first dance with a sore heart. Penelope
alone excepted. The latter, indeed, looks lovely—so
does Gladys—radiant, a very Aurora, true emblem
of the morn—with Nan they make a perfect trio.
' The Delaney girls,' as they are still often called, in
spite of Nan's preferment, carry all before them, until
even Mrs. Dyson-Dwyer, whose charms are great, if
of another order, and who is as scantily attired as the
law will permit, grinds her pretty teeth with envy.
That big hussar had been her special prey for some
time, and now, at a word, a kindly glance from Nan,
he has revolted, and flung her yoke from him. A
tiresome boy, no doubt, although a rich one, and now
of significance, as a first defaulter.

Nan has been good enough to grant him a second dance later on. When it is over she dismisses him with a soft little smile—one of Nan's own—and is preparing to grant herself a small short lounge when the second door leading into the library—the door behind her—opening suddenly, causes her to look round, perhaps a trifle impatiently.

It is Hume.

Something in his face tells her he has not come here by chance. There is purpose in his expression.

'You are not dancing this?' says he, approaching her and speaking in that absent tone that people use when making up their minds as to how best to come at the subject that is occupying them.

'No,' says she idly, 'though I suppose I should be. I am engaged for it to Boyle, but there is plenty of time; he is sure to find me presently.'

'Sure,' says Hume impressively. He trifles with the ornaments on the table for a moment, and then says abruptly, 'I have come here to say something to you.'

'Well, you look like that,' says Mrs. Hume.

'Meet me kindly, Nan,' says he. 'It is not an

easy thing to say because you may—indeed it seems
natural that you must misunderstand me, and yet
I know you don't care for Ffrench. But—it is this
—I wish you would dance no more with him to-
night.'

'Why?' says she, not troubling herself to rise
from her chair, but craning round her soft white
throat that she may get a good look at him.

'Because,' says he, seating himself on the edge of
the table and looking as intently back at her, 'I
cannot bear that people should misjudge you.'

'People don't,' says she.

'I'm afraid they do.'

Thinking of Penelope, Nan grows silent after
this. Certainly Penelope doubts her. But why?
Why? What in the world is the matter with them
all?

'Then they ought to be ashamed of themselves,'
says she at length—rather childishly—as it leads up
to nothing.

'Somebody ought, certainly,' says he gloomily.

'Then it is you,' replies she promptly.

'Or you. Is it kind, do you think, to torture me

as you do? To all the world you are graciousness itself, to me alone you are without feeling. Yet I alone, perhaps, of all the world, love you so entirely, that I have no hope beyond you.'

' I think you should not speak to me like this,' says she, rising at last in a hurried, unnerved way, and going straight up to him. ' You know you shouldn't do it,' says she, laying her hand upon his arm. ' There are women who marry men, pretending that they love them, whilst their hearts are in reality their own—or someone else's; but you should remember that I never deceived you. I gave no love; I expect that no love shall be given me.'

' But, Nan, that is impossible,' says he, closing his hand over hers. ' My love was given you long before our marriage. If you mean that I must not speak of it, that is hard indeed. And listen,' tightening his hold on her fingers, ' why can't you learn to care for me; even a little. They say love begets love; but that is a lie, I think. I love you with all my heart and soul; I love you '—with mournful conviction, 'as I think no man ever loved woman before, and yet I can wake no smallest affection in your

breast.   I shall be dead, and you will not know how
well I loved you.'

'Don't,' says she, in a little sudden sharp way,
pulling her hand out of his.

'Don't what?'

'Don't talk of death like that,' petulantly.   'I hate
it.   And what is it you want me to do for you?'

'Not to dance with your cousin again to-night,'
says he.   'I ask this one thing of you ; a small thing
it seems to me.   Will you grant it?'

He has grown very pale, and is reading her face as
though his very life depends upon her answer.

'How can I?' says she restlessly.   'How is it to
be done?   You do not consider me at all.   Can I
having promised him such and such dances, go to him
and say, "I cannot fulfil my engagements, because
my husband objects to my dancing so often with
you?"'

'Pshaw!' says Hume savagely, and turning abruptly
from her.   'Go and dance with him as often as you
like.'

'Now you are in a bad temper,' says Nan angrily.
'And all because——h'm.   Oh, *you*, Boyle!'

'The 13th. Ours, I think,' says Captain Ffrench, coming towards her.

'Yes,' says Nan, with a little glance at her card, the names on which are, for the moment, however wholly illegible.

CHAPTER III.

'Life's opening chapter pleased me well,
 Too hurriedly I turned the page ;
 I spoiled the volume——'

THE night has not been one of unmixed pleasure to Mr. Croker. For the past few months—during which time he has not come near the county Cork—he has been a sad and sorry young man, finding small good in his life. Perhaps he had not known how fond he was of Penelope until the absurd fancy entered his head that Penelope was not for him.

His first fit of ill-temper, which had a large grain of misery in it, worn off, he would have been glad of an excuse to break through the barrier he himself had raised between Penelope and him ; and when Nan's invitation, which was almost a command to attend her ball, reached him, he grasped his opportunity with eagerness, and determined to have it out with Penelope during the evening.

As we have seen, his first meeting with her was a rather unfortunate one, and drove him back upon his former belief. To appeal to her now would be worse than useless ; it was plain that she had thrown him over—if, indeed, she had ever liked him—and given her heart to Ffrench.

During the evening he had, of course, come face to face with her ; had stopped to say a cold word or two—a word so cold as to be hardly courteous, and had assured himself that the vivid crimson that had dyed her face on their meeting, and the unmistakable nervousness, amounting almost to timidity, that had characterized her manner, had all been proofs of her guilt ; he had quite reached the word guilt by that time, stigmatizing her conduct towards him as the basest treachery.

He had sworn to himself he would not ask her to dance, and instead of accepting Nan's kindly invitation for a week, would so arrange that a timely telegram should recall him to town during the course of the following day. This last resolution held good,

but after awhile a disgraceful longing to be alone
with her once more, to hear her voice addressed to
him only, drives him to ask her for a dance, though
self-contempt goads him as he walks deliberately
towards that part of the ballroom where she is now
standing talking to her partner as the waltz draws to
a close.

'May I have the pleasure of the next?' says he in a
distinctly unfriendly tone, not looking at her.

'It's a quadrille,' says Penelope, faintly smiling. 'I
don't mind walking, as a rule, but to do it for public
inspection——'

She stops short, and smiles again, perhaps more
faintly than before. There is something so unkind
in his whole air, that her heart sinks within her.

'You need not dance, if you don't wish it,' says he
coldly, ignoring her poor little attempt at a joke.

'I should like to sit down somewhere,' says Penelope, who has indeed grown very tired.

'Naturally. When one has danced as indefatigably
as you have all the evening, one must of necessity feel
tired.' There is nothing objectionable in the words
themselves, but something in the tone renders them

unpleasant. There is a hint conveyed—a reproach. It is indeed all at once quite plain to her that he is alluding to her many dances with Boyle Ffrench. She lets him lead her into a conservatory, and there sinks on a couch.

'You haven't danced much,' says she uncertainly.

'Not at all. I began the night by feeling tired.' He is speaking moodily. He has seated himself on a chair opposite to her, and, leaning forward with his arms upon his knees, gazes, without seeing it, at the floor. He is thinking of how she looked in that antechamber with Ffrench, when first he saw her to-night. So animated, so happy, so different from what she looks now. It would be a great stretch of the imagination to believe her happy now.

'You have been working very hard,' says Penelope gently. 'We see your name very often in the papers. It—it has been a great pleasure to us to see how rapidly you are getting on.'

'Has it?'

'Yes. Of course. You must know that.'

'There are many things that one should know, and

doesn't. Well, my "getting on," as you call it, has
been no pleasure to me.'

'I don't like to hear you talk like this,' says Penelope, rather tremulously. Has he fallen in love with
some one in Dublin, and has she been unkind to
him? 'And—you won't mind my saying it, will
you?—but you are a little changed, I think, in some
ways.'

'Every way. Do you know,' with a short, un-
mirthful laugh, 'I believe I used to rather fancy
myself in the old days—flattered myself that I was
a good sort of a fellow, but I have outlived all such
vanity. I know myself now to be about the dullest
man alive.'

'You should give up your work for a while. You
should go abroad, and get change of every kind—
climate and people,' says Penelope, with some difficulty. She is now more than ever convinced that
some Dublin girl has been his undoing. 'Perhaps,'
says she sadly, 'I shouldn't talk to you like this;
but you are such an old friend that——' She just
saves herself from breaking down altogether by
stopping abruptly.

'Old bore, rather,' says he indifferently. 'Don't bother yourself about me ; I'll do well enough. And you——' He pauses, and turns his eyes suddenly to hers, as though about to say something, then checks himself and half rises from his seat. 'It is stupid here for you,' he says abruptly. 'Shall I take you back to the ball-room ?'

'If you wish it. I do not find it stupid,' says Penelope very gently, a suspicion of tears in her shining eyes. 'And all old friends are not bores. You should not have said that.'

'True !' said he recklessly. 'There is Ffrench for a brilliant example. He doesn't seem to bore you, and he is an old friend too.'

The attack is so direct, so sudden, so unexpected, that Penelope's usual sweet calm deserts her. Alas, how many of our friends forsake us in the hour of need ! Her very self-possession leaves her.

'Oh, as for Boyle,' she says confusedly. 'He is more than a friend, he is——' she stammers, growing thoroughly unnerved as she sees his brow darkening. 'He is——'

' What ?' demands he fiercely.

' My cousin !' faintly.

' Oh, Penelope ! That you should stoop to dis-simulation,' says Croker, in a choked voice. Yes ; it is all over. It was only a foolish dream at best. Her evident nervousness suggests to him only the idea that she is aware of his feeling for her, and has still the grace to be ashamed of the part she has played. For once—once she had surely let him think that there was hope for him. No woman could have looked at him as she had looked, and not know what she was doing. She had coquetted with him, openly, heartlessly, and is now a little afraid of her work. That is all.

Almost flinging from him the little hand of entreaty she has unconsciously in her misery laid upon his arm, he moves past her, and forgetful of courtesy, of all the rules due to etiquette, walks out of the conservatory, leaving her to find her way back to the dancing-room alone.

No thought of going anywhere, however, occurs to her. Re-seating herself behind a huge myrtle, that makes a sufficient screen to hide her from the observation of casual indroppers, she gives herself up to the unhappiness of the moment.

What had he meant? How had she offended him? He had certainly appeared annoyed at her dancing so often with Ffrench—but why?—and besides if there was that girl in Dublin—that girl has by now become a settled reality. There can be no doubt about her. Anything more like a broken-hearted man than poor Freddy could hardly be imagined. But if she had been unkind, was that a reason for coming down here, and making her, Penelope, miserable? Oh! how could any girl be unkind to him?

Two hot tears falling on her hand rouse her. She shakes them off her dainty glove, and then, with a swift flush of shame, remembers how she had laid that hand upon his arm to detain him, and how he had cast it off. If he had ever loved her, could he have found the heart to do that? No, he never cared for her! And—and if that is so—why—

Quite a heavy shower follows those two first children of the storm that is now raging within her breast.

'Penny!' says Nan's voice in a frightened whisper.

She has come round the myrtle, and seeing Penelope
in tears, grows terrified. Penelope, who hardly ever
cries! The Delaneys are not a weeping family, and
for one member of it to see another crying, is to feel
sure that some serious crisis has arrived. The scolding
she had received in the gallery, and her indignation
thereat, are alike forgotten as she seats herself beside
her sister and slips her arms round her. 'What has
happened?' asks she.

'It is nothing—nothing at all. Nothing, really,'
declares Penelope, mopping up her eyes, and beginning to feel horribly ashamed of herself.

'Nonsense, Pen; as if you would be crying your
eyes out for nothing. You had better tell me all
about it, because I'll make it my business to find it
out. Has it anything to do with Freddy? Yes, it
has. I see it in your deceitful face.'

'If you do, I needn't tell you,' says poor Penelope,
blushing crimson.

'He's out of his mind, I think,' declares Nan
indignantly. 'I met him just now, and of all the
uncivil, unmannerly beings it has ever been my
misfortune to meet with, give me Freddy Croker.

He tore past me like a sky-rocket, as if I had the plague, and when I called to him pretended not to hear. If those are Dublin manners !'

'Oh, let him alone !' cries Penelope. 'I am sure—I know—his heart is broken. He looked and spoke as if he had given up his life. He—— Oh, Nan !'

She lays her arms around her sister's neck, and hides her face out of sight. She is trembling nervously.

'But why?' asks the bewildered Nan. 'Did you refuse him? If you did that, Penny, I must really say, that——'

'Oh, don't; it isn't me. It is another girl !' murmurs Penelope, in an agony of self-abasement.

'Did he say so?'

'No, no. Only it is impossible not to see it. He is so pale, so strange——'

'Tut! Indigestion !' says Mrs. Hume airily. 'He spends his time poking his nose into musty law-books instead of sitting at your feet, and what can you expect? Don't believe a word about that girl. She couldn't hold a candle to you, any way.'

'How can you tell?' mournfully.

'I know it. Pouf! Just show me your equal.
And how he could resist you in that gown. Well !'

'There is one thing,' says Penelope, dissolving
into tears again. 'Whether he loves her or not,
there is one thing positive, he doesn't love me. Oh,
Nan, and I did like him ; I hate myself when I think
of it.'

'There, darling, there now. Don't take it to heart
like that. After all, ducky, what is he? Only a
man.' If she had said 'only a midge' she could
hardly have expressed more clearly her settled contempt for the 'superfluous sex,' as Mr. Dunphie has
it in his charming book ' The Chameleon.'

'I can't feel as you do,' says Penelope, evidently
with regret. 'He used to be the dearest, best of
fellows, and now—— He told me he found no
pleasure even in his profession—his success. He
spoke very strangely. Oh, Nan, don't speak unkindly
of him. He is really——'

'A bear. A perfect bear,' declares Mrs. Hume unflinchingly. 'An unreasoning bear, too. I've come
to the conclusion that all men are mad ; women alone
are sane. Some men hide successfully their insanity,

but I've come upon two to-night who certainly ought to be locked up if only to ensure the public safety. If, however, you still have a hankering after your bear, let me tell you that I am sure he is yours heart and soul at the present moment, in spite of all you say. Now, Penny, do stop crying,' giving her a tender little shake. ' You will spoil your lovely eyes, and ruin my dance. Where shall we all be when the " Beauty " is unpresentable? And to think Freddy should make you so unhappy as this! Oh !' says Mrs. Hume, uplifting her eyes as if to call down the condemnation of all the gods of Olympus, ' what wretches men are !'

CHAPTER IV.

'I have no heart? Perhaps I have not,
  But then you're mad to take offence
  That I don't give you what I have not got ;
  Use you own common-sense.'

*   *   *   *   *

'Let bygones be bygones ;
  Don't call me false, who owned not to be true.'

*   *   *   *   *

IT is several hours later, and the most determined dancer having at last made his adieu, the Castle once more takes on its normal appearance, and sinks into the silence that befits the coming dawn. Hume, passing along one of the corridors on his way to his own room, seeing a light beneath the door of his sister's sitting-room, goes to it and knocks softly.

'Come in,' says Lady Despard softly, yet in a rather surprised tone. 'You!' she says, smiling slightly, and holding out to him a welcoming hand. 'I thought you in bed, George.'

'I thought the same of you,' returns he slowly, as if preoccupied. 'But seeing the light——'

'You came to have a chat with me,' puts in she brightly. 'Well, let us have it. Pull in your chair closer to the fire. I confess I am as far from sleep as you seem to be.'

She draws the small table on which a shaded lamp is resting close to the hearthrug, and then reseats herself in the lounging-chair she had been occupying when he entered. She is still in her ball-dress, but she has removed the jewels from her throat and wrists, and has thrown her fan and gloves upon a sofa near.

'You can look back upon your dance with a grateful heart,' she begins pleasantly, feeling mischief in the air, yet determining to give him his own time. 'I thought it never would have come to an end! A sure sign of its being a thorough success. Some of the girls looked quite aggrieved with their mothers as they said good-night to Nan.'

'Ah, Nan,' says he. She has struck the key-

note evidently, and every fibre of his body responds
to it.

'What a hostess she makes!' says his sister, with
a little imperceptible haste. 'Perfect, I call her.
Not the ugliest, the most impossible girl left out in
the cold. It is quite a gift.' She has thrown herself, almost without intent, into a laudatory vein,
and is about to still further sing the praises of her
sister-in-law, when he stops her.

'Then you really think her perfect?' says he.

'I think she is—well, if not perfect, one of the best
hostesses I know.'

'You are a wonderful woman,' says he with a half
smile. 'You have not yet told me I was a fool.
Indeed, the orthodox "I told you so" seems beyond
you. I am not asking you about your hostess; I am
asking you about your sister. Well, what do you
think of her?'

'I think she is very much prettier than she used
to be.'

'Ingenious, but of no use whatever. Such a
thought as that would not bring such an expression
to your face. Now, what do you think of her?'

'I think she is an accomplished coquette,' says Lady Despard flatly, thus driven to bay.

'You mean——?'

'Hardly anything, really. Only, it seems a pity she should so waste her time. She is lovely. Her manner is very far above even what I had imagined it. She might be an ideal chatelaine, and yet——'

'Well,'—roughly—'go on.'

'That Captain Ffrench,' says his sister, turning quickly towards him. 'What does he do here?'

'He is her cousin,' says Hume calmly, even whilst the icy hand of despair seems to clutch his heart.

'Such cousins are superfluous. He'—with an effort—'fancies himself in love with her.'

'If you think,'—begins he hotly.

'I think nothing—except that the man is a fool—and that sometimes a fool can do great mischief. I think, too, that a man who cannot control himself and his features is very much better out of society.'

'Nan does not care for him,' abruptly.

'Tut! my good George. Who runs may read that.'

'Yet you seemed to me to insinuate——'

'That Captain Ffrench is a superfluity—no more. You know it is a little fad of mine to study my fellow-creatures, and I have studied Captain Ffrench very carefully. I have come to the conclusion that no woman in her senses could possibly compare him with you favourably; Nan is quite in her senses.'

'Thank you,' says Hume, taking her hand and pressing it. Then, 'She does not care for me either.'

'Give her time.'

'She has had a great deal of time.'

'Well?'

'And it has failed me.'

'Are you so sure of that?'

'You can see for yourself.'

'Providentially that is a blessing allowed to most people. Yes, I see. And certainly not with your eyes.'

'How then?' asks he.

'It is the plainest thing. You half believe her in love with her cousin; I know she does not care for him at all.'

'You take a weight off my mind,' says Hume, drawing a long breath. 'I feared you might misunderstand her. After all it is only me you fail to comprehend. You think I doubt her. No! Not for one moment. But I fear the judgment of society— for her sake.'

'You are very much in love with her still,' says his sister, with a half smile.

'Am I? I suppose so. I was always rather a stubborn sort of fellow,' says he, returning her smile with an effort. 'And now, good-night. I have kept you up too long already.'

'You will go to bed, George?'

'It is hardly worth while. And it is useless my thinking of a beauty sleep. Now, get an hour's rest or so.'

He kisses her, and, laughing off her renewed entreaties that he will lie down for a while, descends the staircase, and, throwing himself into an armchair, takes up a book and tries to read.

In vain, however. In spite of his effort to appear satisfied with affairs as they stand when with his sister—in spite, too, of the real satisfaction derived

from the assurance of her full belief in Nan's indifference towards her cousin, he is too sad at heart to
think of anything but that last scene with her, when
she had refused him the one small request he had
made her.

It was a request so small that it seems to him she
would have granted it to almost anyone but him.
She is, indeed, of that nature (Irish nature, be it said,
pur et simple) that finds it difficult to say ' No ' to the
most indifferent of importunates. And to give up a
dance with anyone to please another, would have
been but a small matter with her ; yet to him she
had been adamant. It seems plain to him in this
hour that, if she likes no man, there is still one man
whom she cordially dislikes. Her own words rush
back upon him. She had said she hated him. He
had put it down then to the natural anger of a girl
placed by no fault of her own (or of his either for
the matter of that) in a false position. He had
not quite believed it. Perhaps, after all, it was the
truth.

A knock at the door ; not a nervous or a
deferential knock, a decided little rat-a-tat-tat, that

puts an end to his moody meditation on the spot.
No one but Nan could have made such a vigorous
assault as that upon his door at this unearthly hour.
Not waiting for an answer, the author of the knock
throws open the door, and there stands Nan sure
enough.

A delightful Nan, with her eyes as bright, her air
as insouciant as though she had been sleeping the
sleep of the just all night instead of dancing holes in
her stockings. She has on her sauciest expression
and the very daintiest of white peignoirs, all laces
and frills and furbelows, and with white fur ruffles at
the throat and wrists. Her dark gray eyes look black
as she stands in the shadow of the doorway, and all
the little soft curls of her hair seem to have shaken
themselves loose.

'Can I come in ?' asks she, making a pretence at
hesitating on the threshold.

'I really don't see why you need put that question,'
replies he coldly. 'You are in, aren't you ?'

'Only just,' says Mrs. Hume, with a backward
glance at the half open door. 'Well, I'm glad to see
you are not so hermetically sealed up as usual—that

one can effect an entrance occasionally. Can I speak
to you for a moment? Can you,' with a half laughing, half defiant glance at him, 'spare me so much of
your valuable time?'

It is plain she has not come as a penitent. She
seems to hold herself in the highest esteem, and
to be as pleased with herself as possible.

'I don't see why you need ask permission to do
that either,' says Mr. Hume, standing with his back
to the chimney-piece and surveying her grimly.
'You don't as a rule hesitate about saying to me anything that is in your mind, no matter how hurtful it
may be. Don't break through your usual habit to-
night, I beg of you. I'm prepared for anything.
Though what you can have to say to me does, I
confess, puzzle me. A folly on my part! as I ought
to have learned by this to be astonished at nothing
that you can do.'

'I'll astonish you this time, at all events,' says
Nan triumphantly; 'I've come,' pausing as if to
make the final effect greater, 'to beg your pardon!
There!'

'Eh?'

She laughs gaily.

'Ah! I thought that would do it. Yes, really. For once in my life, you see, I have done the right thing. It's old-fashioned to go down on one's knees, or else I'd do that too. Now listen. George, I beg your pardon !'

'For what?' asks Hume, with very pardonable astonishment.

'For having danced with Boyle when you asked me not to do it. Now,' seeing him about to speak. 'I'm not going a bit farther into it ; and I'm not going to be at all sorry about it, so it is no use your cross-examining me.'

'I don't believe you are sorry at all,' says Hume, with a frown.

'Then you are wrong, most sapient judge. I suffered for my incivility to you, I can tell you. Boyle was in a temper that would not have disgraced a Bluebeard. I'm certain he wanted to chop my head off, so you see you were amply avenged.'

'I don't in the least care how he felt,' says Hume harshly, flinging the cigarette he has been holding into the fire.

'You don't seem to care how I feel either,' says Nan. 'Do you know it is winter, and that standing about a hundred miles from a fire is not conducive to comfort? You might offer me a chair I think.'

'I beg your pardon,' says Hume, who had in truth forgotten everything, even his manners, which as a rule are exceedingly good, in his anger and surprise and discomfiture at her unexpected coming. 'See, this chair is comfortable; I'm afraid you must be half frozen.'

'I'm not as warm as I might be certainly. What a good fire,' opening wide all her ten pretty fingers and stretching them over the grateful warmth. 'You do take care of yourself I must say. Well,' looking up at him from the depths of a cosy chair, 'it wasn't altogether to beg your pardon I came either. It was to tell you something that ought to make you a happy man for life.'

'There is only one thing could make me that,' says Hume, with admirable readiness. It should have won him his reward, but it doesn't.

'Oh, well, it isn't that,' returns Nan naïvely. 'Something, however, almost as good. I've come to

tell you'—with solemnity befitting the occasion—
'that our poor, unfortunate, ill-tempered Boyle is in
love——' She makes a tragic pause.

'Once for all——' begins Hume angrily, but is
here interrupted in his turn.

'If you would have the courtesy to hear me out,
says she airily, 'without meaningless bursts of
pleasantry, you would probably be able to gather the
exact drift of my tale. He is in love—said I—not
with me, but with Penelope.'

Hume stares at her. It is impossible to accuse
her of duplicity. She looks, indeed, quite delighted
with her disclosure, and folding her hands over her
crossed knees, nods her head at him several times
with all the air of one who has gained a distinct
triumph.

'It is true,' says she, 'so your mind may be at rest
about me. Come now, am I not amiability itself?
In spite of that horrid scolding you gave me this
evening, first thing I do when I make my discovery
is to come here and tell you all about it. And
another thing, it isn't the easiest of tales to tell. For
me there is humiliation in it. No woman likes to

say her lover is no longer her lover, and yet I have braved even that.'   .

'And pray when did you make this remarkable discovery, as you call it ?'

'I've been making it for a good while,' says Mrs. Hume, with much aplomb. 'Bit by bit it has dawned upon me, but to-night—don't you think he seemed very fond of her to-night ?'

'No, I don't,' says Hume.

'Well, of course you wouldn't,' says Nan, after a disappointed pause. 'You're a man. Didn't you notice how he looked at her ?'

'No. I noticed how he looked at you though.'

'It didn't even occur to you, I suppose, how often he danced with her ?'

'It occurred to me that he danced with her just as often as he was unfortunate enough not to be able to gain a dance from you. And that was not so very often.'

Mrs. Hume, planting her elbow on her knee, lets her chin sink into the pink palm of one hand, and from that charming resting-place looks up at him.

'Same old game!' says she mournfully. 'I wonder you don't grow tired of it.'

'I wonder you don't! Considering Captain Ffrench's very limited conversational powers, I should think you must be thoroughly bored by this time.'

'Then you don't believe he is in love with Penelope? You still persist in thinking he is— is——'

'Yes. I really think he still is.'

'Then you are as stupid as he is,' angrily.

'How is he stupid?'

'Because, for the second time, he has given his heart to a woman who cares nothing at all for him.'

Hume turns abruptly away, and pretends to busy himself with the fire. He is almost ashamed to let her see how her words have affected him. The quick rush of glad blood to his brow, the light that he knows has come into his eyes, both must have betrayed him. With a thorough belief in her indifference for Ffrench, it is still unspeakable happiness to him to hear her declare it aloud like this.

34—2

'Besides,' goes on Nan presently, who has evidently in the meantime been studying the question, 'if he still was in love with me, as you foolishly persist in saying, I suppose,' regarding him with determined question in her eye, 'he'd say something to me about it.   Eh ?'

'I really haven't studied him,' says Hume, his brow darkening.

'Well, he doesn't, anyway,' declares Nan, in a tone that is evidently meant to settle the matter.

'And what does he say to Penelope ?' asks Hume, with a faint sneer.

'That I don't know.'

'As little as he says to you, no doubt.   He seems a modest youth.'

'Do you know,' says Mrs. Hume, regarding him with crushing pity, 'I wouldn't be as narrow-minded as you are, for anything you could offer me.'

She looks so lovely and so entirely without temper in her small attempt at impertinence, that Hume gives way a little, and comes down off his stilts.

'Let us think as you do by all means,' says he, with a slight laugh. 'There is one more question, however, I should like to put to you. What does Penelope say to him?'

'Ah, that is the cruel part of it. She doesn't care for him at all. Not the smallest little bit in the world. Poor fellow! And she is so pretty, and it will be such a disappointment. Even though you don't like him, it is impossible but you must feel some regret for him. Think,' earnestly, 'what a terrible thing it must be to love someone, and then find that that "someone" doesn't care for you at all!'

'Nan!' His voice is so abrupt, so charged with anger that almost outdoes the pain in it, that Nan starts and rises confusedly to her feet. He has grown very pale, and is looking at her with passionate reproach in his eyes.

'Oh! I didn't mean that. I didn't indeed,' says she nervously. 'I never thought of it. You know I always say the wrong thing. And—and besides, you are different. You—have been able to marry me. I belong to you. I am yours——'

She breaks off as if not knowing how to go on, with those condemnatory eyes on hers.

'You are mine,' repeats he; 'and can you say so? You belong to me, indeed—but how? Bound to me against your will—hating me always——'

'Oh no, not hating,' says Nan anxiously.

'Is that true, Nan?' going up to her, and throwing his arm round her; 'if indeed you no longer hate me, why, why can't you learn to love me?'

'I don't know,' says Nan rather nervously, and moving very uneasily within his embrace, as if afraid of something. 'That's it, you see. I don't know.'

'But why don't you? What's the matter with me that you can't love me? I am not an unkind or a cross fellow, am I?' In his eagerness to defend himself he tightens the arm that is holding her, very slightly but decidedly.

'N—n—o,' says Mrs. Hume, making a more decided effort to escape. 'That is, not exactly; one might think—what I mean is—' It is quite plain by this time that she doesn't in the least know what she means. 'It is this,' says she desperately—'you can be cross at times, you know.'

'If I ever have been, I'm sorry for it,' says he

honestly, bending down to see what effect this apology will have upon her. His action, at all events, has a very remarkable effect ; breaking from him by a sharp and violent effort, she stands away from him, her breath coming hurriedly from between her parted lips.

'What's the matter ?' asks he, all at once guessing the meaning of her sudden fear.

'I—you—I thought you were going to kiss me. Don't ever kiss me !' says she imperiously. 'I—I shall hate you all over again, if you do.'

'I wasn't going to kiss you,' says he indignantly.

'Well, you looked like it,' says she, with open disbelief.

'My looks belied me then. I have no desire whatever to kiss you,' says Hume coldly.

A long and deadly pause. Suddenly, as if finding it impossible to suppress herself any longer, Mrs. Hume bursts out laughing.

'Haven't you ?' says she. 'Are you sure ?' A moment ago she had seemed to shrink from him ; now beyond the dangerous circle of his arm all the old bravery returns to her, and with it the saucy daring that, rightly or wrongly, must be considered one of her greatest charms. 'Do you mean to tell me,' cries she, dancing up to him with her slender fingers embracing her waist, and with her head a little held on one side, 'that if now, this instant, I were to ask you to kiss me, you would refuse? Come. Come now! The truth, the truth, and nothing but the truth.'

Hume, who is struggling with a wild and disgraceful desire to laugh with her, and thus give in to her humour, pauses to think of a crushing reply, but pauses so long that she in her present audacious mood cannot wait for it.

'Pouf!' says she airily. 'You needn't say it. No one would believe you. No one knows better than you, that if I were to hold out even one finger to you,' adorning this remark by poking at him a slim forefinger, 'you would be down on your knees to me in a moment.'

'I don't see why you need take such pride in that thought,' says Hume calmly, who has now succeeded in conquering the aforesaid disgraceful longing. 'I've been at your feet for so many months, that the novelty of the situation ought to have been worn through by this time.' Then, abruptly, 'Do you know what hour it is, that even the wintry dawn has come to us at last? Don't you want to get some sleep?'

She shakes her head.

'I never was less tired in my life. I feel as if I should never want to go to sleep again. By-the-bye,' leaning on the top of a tall *prie-dieu*, and looking at him over it, 'your incubus is going to be lifted off your shoulders almost immediately. It is,' glancing at the clock, 'half-past six now, and Boyle will be leaving this at seven.'

'Is that why you won't go to bed?' gravely. 'Do you wish to give him an adieu?'

'Well, I thought of it. I asked Penelope if she would see him off—he looked so disconsolate—but she refused. However, if you——'

'I am not going to ask a favour of you again,' coldly.

'Another way of doing it,' returns she, laughing. 'I grant it this time. I told you I was in an amiable mood, did I not? You shall be obeyed, my lord. He

shall go out into the wide wide world without a
parting word from me—old friend though he is. As
for me,' with a little yawn, ' I'll go and have a bath,
I think.'

' Have a sleep first,' says Hume kindly.   ' You will
find the day too long if you don't.'

' And you ?'

' I'll take my own advice,' says he, rising and
smiling at her. ' Good-night. Good-morning, rather.'

' Good-bye is as good as either.'

' Oh no.   Much sadder.'

' Is that why you wish to spare it to Boyle ?' asks
she, making him a charming little grimace. And
just at the door, when she has got beyond it indeed,
she cannot resist thrusting her head in again to say
a last teasing word. ' Be sure you dream of me,'
says she, with a little nod, and runs up the stairs
singing.

Hume stands at the table, drumming idly upon it
with one hand, lost in thought. Presently he lifts his
head.

' She could not look like that and be unhappy,'
says he slowly. ' Thank God for that, at least.'

CHAPTER V.

'WELL,' says Mr. Murphy, the morning after the ball, laying down the tray he has brought into the small room that serves as boudoir, working-room, and den for Gladys and Penelope, ''twas a thrate to see ye last night!' So much flattery given to the children he has sedulously repressed all his life seems to be too much for him, and he is silent for a moment. Only for a moment. 'Oh!' says he, still further forgetting his principles, and speaking with all the air of one who must declare his real sentiments or die, 'to look at ye! 'Twas boilin' wid envy was ivery other mother's sowl of thim in the room.'

At this, Penelope and Gladys, who had elected to have their late breakfast here, and who had been looking pensive, as girls will when a long-expected

pleasure has at last been fulfilled and only the ashes
of it remain, pluck up sufficient heart to break into
irrepressible laughter.

'Ah, Murphy, at last you see it!' cries Penelope.
'What years it has taken you! We are the loveliest
girls in the world—we are—we are!'

'To spake like that is unbecomin',' says Mr.
Murphy austerely. 'That's bould boastin'. Ye
should thank the Lord if ye have dacent fatures—
though,' prudently, 'ye shouldn't be too sure of that,
ayther, as it's only a poor ould ignorant man that
tells ye so—an' not give yerselves airs about it. But
what I was goin' to say, miss,' with a return to his
former geniality, as he feels his duty was performed,
'is this: Did ye iver see so grand a ball? 'Twas a
credit to the county, that's what I call it. Crack
yer egg now, miss, an' ate a bit. 'Tis half kilt ye
must be.'

'Oh, Murphy, weren't the rooms lovely?' says
Gladys. 'Such flowers! And the band and all.
'Twas my first ball, you know; and if they are all
like that——'

She finishes up with a sigh of utter content.

' 'Twas mine, too, miss,' says Mr. Murphy solemnly. 'An' I tuk great pride out of it. Ye know yerself I wouldn't have been there at all if Miss Nan an' Misther Hume hadn't axed me theirselves, an' made a rale request of it.' It is easy to see that the old man is actually bursting with the 'great pride he tuk out of it.' 'An' only for the grand new shuit that Misther Hume gave me I couldn't have dared to show me nose there, wid thim London blagguards o' servants ready to run down a respectable man, just because he hasn't got a bran-new coat to his back.'

'You looked lovely, Murphy!' says Penelope sweetly. 'Don't stand there : sit down and talk to us about the ball for a bit.'

She can see that he is tired from his loss of sleep, though excitement, that is all pleasurable, still keeps his eyes as bright as though he were seven instead of seventy.

'Thank ye kindly, miss, an' if I may take the liberty.'

He seats himself gingerly upon a chair, and looks happily at these two of his children, as, with un-checked appetites, they get through their breakfast.

Penelope, in truth, is sad at heart, but when one is young, hunger ever follows upon grief.

' 'Twas a great sight intirely,' says he ; ' 'twas in me heart all night that I wished the poor misthress could a' seen it. Whin I saw Miss Nan standin' at the top of the room as proud as a Begum, faix, an wid all the Hume jools in her hair, I thought I'd a' died. Glory be, sich diamonds! 'Twas a grand sight for an ould fool like me. An' Misther Hume himself ; he's the rale sort, he is ! There's a gentle-man if ye like, bone an' muscle.'

' Yes, yes ; one must like him,' says Penelope, and then stops short, as if she feels she has been unfaithful to Nan.

' I love him,' says Gladys, without reservation of any sort.

' An' so ye well might, me dear. Where's his like, I'd ask ye ? Look here now, miss, I'll tell ye a thing about him. I was in the supper-room one time, pur-tendin', ye know,' with a wave of his hand, ' to be busy at wan o' the tables, but only thinkin', faix, of the beautiful sight before me, when up comes hisself, an' gives me a nate slap on the back. " Well,

Murphy," says he, as pleasant as ye plaze, for all the world, indeed, as if I'd been wan o' the guests, " an' how are you gettin' on ?" says he. " Oh, first rate, sir," says I, an' on he wint. But tell me now, Miss Penelope, wasn't that great notice to take of an ould man like me ? Oh, faith, he's straight all through, is Hume !'

'It is just the sort of thing he would do,' says Gladys. ' I think he has the kindest eyes I ever saw. But, Murphy, didn't Mrs. Hume look lovely?'

'Arrah, don't ye be talkin'! Who would ye compare wid her, at all at all ?'

'Not one,' says Penelope, rousing herself from a rather sad little dream.

'Was she the belle ?' asks Gladys uncertainly. ' That Mrs. Dyson-Dwyer—her red hair gave her a sort of look——'

'Yes. But I didn't like the look,' says Penelope.

' Are ye talkin' of ould Dan Connell's daughter ?' asks Mr. Murphy suddenly, with terrible disdain in his tone. ' An' is it comparin' her wid Miss Nan ye'd be ? The saints forgive ye! That ondacent girl. An' not one dhrop ov the rale blood in her body.'

'Oh, nonsense, Murphy! Her husband is——'

'I don't care a thrawneen for her husband. Yer husband can't give ye blood, nor make a lady of ye,' says this determined old aristocrat disdainfully. 'I mind ould Dan Connell well, an' the time he came here to this village, when the collidge below was called only a school, an' he was wan ov the tutors in it. He wouldn't live inside ov it, mind ye, for he was too fond o' the dhrop, an', o' course, he couldn't git it there; so he took rooms in the village, the ould varmint!'

'Why, what on earth did he do to you, Murphy, to make you so bitter?'

'Nothing, miss, not a ha'porth, but I hate that low lot,' says Mr. Murphy, pinching up his lips.

'Are you sure Mrs. Dyson-Dwyer's father was only a tutor?' asks Penelope. 'She looks as if——'

'He might a' bin a Dook,' suggests Mr. Murphy. 'She do indeed, miss. But I knows all about her, an' that's what maddens me when I hear Miss Gladys compare her wid our Miss Nan. Why, that father of hers, Dan Connell, he lodged, as I tell ye, in the village down below, with the Dempseys; an' whin he

had been there for five months, wid niver a farthin'
paid for anythin', an' the grog and the punch ordhered
galore, he suddenly disappeared.'

'What! spirited away? That must have been
pungent whisky,' says Gladys.

'Well, he went away, anyhow; and whin the third
day came round, an' no sign of him, Pat Dempsey
went up to his room an' stove in the door, and sure
enough there was a clane sweep made of iverything,
barrin' his big thrunk, that stood in the corner. It
was locked, an' it was mortial heavy; not a man
amongst 'em could move it; so they tuk great comfort
out of that thrunk, an' wint downstairs agin, an' determined to wait till the end o' the week before doin'
anything. For even if he had run away, says they to
thimselves, widout payin' his bill, why, the contints of
that heavy thrunk would recompinse thim over an'
over agin.'

'Why, what did they think was in it?'

'Why, clothes, miss, to be sure, an' maybe valables
o' one sort or another, 'twas so terrible hard to move.
Well,' continues Mr. Murphy, crossing one leg over
the other, and giving himself up more entirely to the

interest of his tale. 'The week came to an end, an'
up the stairs wint Pat Dempsey an' his wife an' the
whole family, armed wid a crowbar to bust open the
thrunk. 'Twas a hard job, for 'twas powerfully
tightly closed, but at long last up flew the lid,
and——'

'Yes? Well? What did they find?' asks Gladys
eagerly, who has been working herself up to a pitch
of excitement that nothing will appease save the dead
body of Dan Connell himself in that thrilling trunk.

'Divil a thing, me dear—savin' yer presence—
except the four tenpenny nails wid which he had
fastened the thrunk to the floor! Oh, murdher! but
ye should a' heard the Dempseys thin. Sich
screechin' an' yellin'. I'm tould ye'd a' heard thim
in Glandore. Glory be! was there iver sich a take-
in——'

Here Mr. Murphy gives way to the delight that is
overpowering him. Spreading out his shrivelled old
hands on his knees, he laughs and laughs again, the
silver merriment of the two girls joining in with his
ancient cackle.

'So there's ould Connell for ye,' says he at

last. 'And he was own father to Mrs. Dyson-Dwyer.'

'Oh, but it seems impossible,' says Gladys, re-calling the beauty of last night.

'Faith so it do, miss. An' ye'd think it sthranger still if ye'd iver seen ould Connell himself; wid his nose like a live coal, an' a mouth big enough to do jooty for the whole family. But her mother was a nate little woman enough, an' she had a brother who made a big fortin in Austhraly, an' he left it all to her daughther; and the daughther turnin' out to have a pretty face of her own, Misther Dyson-Dwyer saw her, an' fell in love wid her, an' there she is now, faix, holdin' up her head with the best o' thim this day. The world's a quare place entirely,' says Mr. Murphy, with a sigh for its eccentricities. 'Down to-day an' up to-morrow is the way of it.'

The words seem to touch Penelope. She pales a little and pushes away her plate. Truly the world is a sorry place—with small happiness in it.

'I wonder if Mrs. Dyson-Dwyer knows about that trunk?' says Gladys pensively. 'Did they ever re-cover it? I suppose it might be considered by this

35—2

time in the light of an heirloom. Who's that?' as a knock comes to the door. 'Oh, you, William! Have some breakfast,' hospitably.

'Breakfast!' says William the Gruff, regarding his sisters with deep disgust. 'It would be decenter to give it another name at this hour! What lazy things girls are! No, thank you. Tea and eggs at one o'clock. Bah! Murphy, father wants you! He says Miss Penelope is letting the house go to the dogs, and that he can't get his sherry because the keys are mislaid.'

'The keys! good gracious, where are they?' cries Penelope, starting up. 'Nolly, have you them?' as Norah appears in the doorway.

'I think I know where they are,' says that smart little damsel, and galloping off soon returns with them breathless: 'I have them. Here's the keys,' exclaims she triumphantly, holding them out.

'What English that child does speak, to be sure!' says Penelope, who is out of sorts with all the world. 'Don't say, "Here is the keys," Norah; say, "Here are the keys."'

'I didn't say, "Here is the keys," says Nolly indignantly. ' I said, " Here's the keys !" You heard me, Gladys ?'

At this both Gladys and William roar with laughter.

' Come here, Nolly ; you shall have two lumps of sugar for that,' cries Gladys. ' Best of grammarians, you are indeed worth your weight in gold. Here, Penny ! Here's the keys, go and give your father his sherry !'

CHAPTER VI.

'Thou only hast stepped unaware,
 Malice not one can impute ;
And why should a heart have been there
 In the way of a fair woman's foot?'

* * * * *

OLD Winter lies dead at last, and young Spring, lusty and strong, is running about all over the land. High and far his voice resounds, as through the woodlands, and up from the valley below, rushes the musical pipings of a thousand birds. Everywhere

'The song of thrush or linnet
 Greets thee from the hawthorn bough.'

And the soft beatings of their wings, as joyously they fly from branch to branch, adds to the general jubilee.

It is the twenty-ninth of March. Two more days will see capricious April safely installed in the seat of honour. And the bolder month, feeling its dissolution so close at hand, has all suddenly grown meek and laid down his arms, and ceased the wild bluster that has distinguished him during his earlier days. He is indeed 'going out like a lamb.' Anything milder or more harmless than this last day of his can hardly be imagined. It is warm, sweet, and scented, like a June hour.

Nan, whose guests have all departed long ago, and who is just now feeling time hang rather heavy on her hands, has started to walk through the woods of Hume down to her old home. A faint recollection of that day—long past now—when she had gone up to Hume with William to intercede with its master for that erring youth, returns to her. How little she had thought then that Fate was following hard upon her heels that day, and that only time was wanted to make her that master's wife !

The recollection is so slight, and so undesired, that she flings it from her, as one in which danger may dwell—danger to the full enjoyment of this most glorious day.

There is positive warmth in the clear sunshine that strikes on budding tree and flower. The fern fronds are thrusting out their delicate mossy heads, as though eager to begin life as soon as possible. The heavens are cloudless; the whole air one fragrant breath from the violets and primroses that throng her path. The boy Spring—wild, exultant— is holding high carnival in the woods of Hume this day.

Nan, pausing, looks around her. All at once the freshness, the sweetness of everything she sees reminds her in some unexplainable way of Penelope— Penelope as she used to be. A pang shoots through her heart as she thinks of the Penelope of to-day—so changed, so still, so silent. A lovely Penelope always, but with the old glad life and heart and spirit gone out of her.

She did not feel well, she said yesterday, when Nan had put her through a stiff cross-examination ; whereupon Nan had formulated a plan that should carry her off to town with them—she and Hume—

when they started in May to spend the season in London. But in the meantime why should Penelope look like that—as if the world was so poor a place that she would fain be out of it ? What could be the matter with her ? Oh, if it was Freddy !

Nan stamps her foot upon the ground as she comes to this point in her thoughts, and tells herself she hates Freddy Croker.

Since that night, at her own ball, she had never seen him. He had not come near the country. He was given up body and soul to the making of a name for himself at the Bar, and just at present somebody had told her he was abroad. So was Boyle, by the way.

A rabbit twinkling through the bracken at her feet rouses her, and sets her once more in motion. It is now close upon three o'clock, and the soft spring days as yet are short, and it is rather a long walk to Rathmore and back again : she must make haste. Yet how difficult to go swiftly by all the beauties that nature has so lavishly flung into her way ! Down there, with the sun glittering on it, lies the lake—one huge diamond as the light now lies, and as she watches it, with her hand lifted to her forehead, a stately heron rises majestically, and sails slowly, slowly southwards.

A tiny brown bird, with a sharp twitter, flies from the branch on her right almost to her feet, in quest of a witless worm—greedy thing!—and Nan's eyes follow it, lose it, only to gain something else, so generous is this warm spring-time. The bird is gone, but here to her eyes is spread a whole carpet of flowers, coloured, as dyer never yet could paint his clothes.

> ' Heigh-ho ! daisies and buttercups,
> Fair yellow daffodils, stately and tall ;
> A sunshiny world, full of laughter and leisure,
> And fresh hearts, unconscious of sorrow and thrall.
> Send down on their pleasure smiles passing its measure,
> God that is over us all.'

Yes. Boyle has gone abroad too. A run over to Paris, nothing more than that. But, thank goodness, he is out of the way. He has grown almost insupportable of late—with his gloomy looks, cause unknown—and everybody else's gloomy looks about him, cause very well known. If he is in love with Penelope, why on earth doesn't he say so, and put an

end to the annoying conclusion to which her husband
and Penelope herself have come, that he is idiotic
enough to be still in love with her—Nan?

Ridiculous folly! Ridiculous, repeats Mrs. Hume
to herself as she walks along, and yet there is something in the obstinacy with which she clings to this
word that frightens her. Once again she stops in
her walk, forgetful of the still short days, as a hateful doubt creeps into her mind—not for the first
time. If George and Penelope should be right, and
she herself wrong! If it should be proved positively,
that Boyle still thinks of her, as in those old dead
days—how then? A sensation of actual fear seizes
on her as she lets this idea gain room—fear mingled
with disgust. Raising her eyes, that have been fixed
upon the earth, towards heaven, as if to free herself
from this detestable supposition, she suddenly finds
herself face to face with Captain Ffrench.

CHAPTER VII.

'For ever changing, still you rove,
  As I in boyhood roved ;
  But when you tell me this is love,
  It proves you never loved !'

'YOU !' says she. The dislike to her late fancy has not yet died from her face, and there is altogether a disgraceful lack of courtesy in the greeting she offers him. When she had believed him so happily far away—so unlikely to trouble her peace again—to find him thus suddenly before her, fills her with a sort of unreasoning and decidedly unjust anger.

'Nothing better !' returns he morosely, enraged by her evident annoyance at his presence. 'To judge by your looks, one might think me the fiend himself in person.'

'Why, Julia told me you were in Paris,' says she indignantly.

'Well, so I was,' doggedly. 'I returned last night, and came down here this morning.'

'You needn't tell me that,' with unmitigated resent-ment. 'I can see you. Good heavens !' pushing back the riotous locks from her forehead, and growing even more incensed. 'What a bad halfpenny you are— turning up at all hours, and just when least expected ! How do you manage it ? I never heard of anyone in all my life who could get so much leave as you do.'

'So much !'

'So very, very much ! In my humble opinion the duties of the British soldier may be regarded as a screaming farce.'

'I don't know what you mean,' says Ffrench, trying to speak with a proper calm. 'I have not been down here since Christmas. If you think——'

'Well, what brings you now ?' interrupts she with quite remarkable rudeness, and with that sense of injury still full upon her.

'You certainly are in a very extraordinary mood,' says he, his eyes on the ground, his cane busily en-gaged in the decapitation of the delicate daisies at his feet. It seems to give him a sort of savage pleasure to see them lying dead and dying on the short young grass. 'Why should I not be here?'

'Why, indeed? Still, answer me,' says she with so direct a look, with such a fresh young growth of angry suspicion in her eyes, that he quails. The old first dissimulation that he had almost cast aside as useless now returns to him.

'You might guess,' he says, his dark face again bent earthwards.

'I couldn't,' says Nan impatiently. There is just a little touch of hauteur in her manner, a certain dangerous light in her eyes that warns him to give a decisive answer—and at once.

'Is not Penelope here?' says he in a low tone, and without looking at her.

'Penelope?' She repeats her sister's name again, as if to make sure she has heard aright. Perhaps, after all, in spite of the ardent manner in which she had tried to persuade herself into a belief in it, she had not altogether credited that idea of his being in love with Penelope. There is astonishment in her tone as she speaks—and not only that, but a little irrepressible incredulity, and something else that might resolve itself into relief. There is almost every note in it indeed, except chagrin.

'But Penelope,' begins she, thinking with consternation of that scene at her own dance, where Penelope had laid bare to her her heart. 'If he is in earnest what can she say to him now? Have you spoken to her?' asks she softly.

'No.'

'I am afraid. . . . Oh! Boyle,' an expression of honest grief and regret saddening her features. 'Are you really going to tell me that you have fallen in love with Penelope?'

'Why?' says he, in a husky voice, dwelling with a mad hope on that sudden change in her. 'Would you—care?'

'Oh, you know I would,' cries she, the tears starting to her eyes. Poor fellow, if he is really in earnest, how is she to explain it all to him?

'Has—has it never occurred to you,' falters she, 'that——'

'What?' his dark, eager eyes still devouring her sorrowful face.

'That Penelope——' She hesitates. It is so

difficult to speak without betraying Penelope's secret, without once again hurting his *amour propre;* 'I don't think Penelope cares for you in that way,' says she at last, driven to bluntness because of her inability to think of anything else in her present nervous state.

Ffrench stares at her. Has she really believed him then? And her hesitation, her evident agitation, is it jealousy? A dull man in many ways, and vain to a degree, as dull men often are, blinded too by his own passion for her that has never slumbered or slept, he clings now to this wild fancy, and feeds upon it with a sudden fierce vigour that shows how hungered he has been for such food for many days—how near to starvation he has come through lack of it.

'Of course I can't be sure,' she goes on quickly, awkwardly as he tells himself, though the awkwardness arises from a very different cause to that which he ascribes to it. 'It is impossible to judge of anybody's feelings. People change so.'

'Some people don't,' says he, in a tone so curious that involuntarily she looks at him.

'True,' says she slowly, feeling a little puzzled and with doubt growing strong within her once more. 'But such people are so rare that we seldom meet them.'

'You should be the last to say that. You at least have met one,' says he, this time hurriedly.

A little sinking at the heart admonishes Nan to laugh, and make light of this new inexplicable mood that has seized hold of him.

'You mean Mr. Hume,' says she lightly. 'Yes. He looks like that.'

'Does he?' sullenly. 'I was not thinking of him.'

'Of yourself, then?' looking him full in the eyes. 'So much the better for Penelope, if she chooses to listen to you. By-the-bye, I am going to Rathmore now—will you accompany me?'

'Not now. I shall go there later on,' says he carefully. That one irrepressible outburst had almost betrayed him, but now he has himself well under control again. It is better, no doubt, to have this shadow—this vague figure of Penelope between them, until he can with safety say to her, what she

already knows is in his heart. During all the long
months since her marriage, in spite of the silence he
has compelled himself to keep, the certainty that
she understood was never away from him. The
knowledge that she had wedded Hume against her
will had become clear to him shortly after her return
to the Castle; and that knowledge once entered into
him, all things else seemed plain. She did not love
Hume. She had loved him. A malign fate had
tried to separate her from him, but fate had been
defied before now, and could, nay, should be defied
again.

'You are staying with Julia,' says Nan, who is
making conversation very diligently.

'Yes. In spite of her many excellent qualities,'
says Boyle sneeringly, 'it has occurred to me at
times that Julia is a somewhat superfluous person.'

'You should not say that. She has been very
kind,' says Nan, making her rebuke in a singularly
kind tone, so great is her pity for him. Once again
she has veered round to the belief that he has now
foolishly given all the affection of which he is capable
into Penelope's unsympathetic keeping.

"'Tis a killing kindness,' says he. 'I don't know anything that I would not rather do than spend an evening alone with Julia.'

'I suppose all aunts are unpleasant,' says Nan, with a sigh. 'Well—as the prospect of an evening seems to weigh so heavily on you, come up to Hume, and spend it with us. Mr. Hume will be very glad if you will dine with us.'

'Thank you,' stiffly. The invitation would have been more welcome if Hume's name had not been introduced. But then he tells himself it was always one of Nan's charms to throw a touch of dignity into all she said and did. She would no doubt acknowledge Hume's claim on her until the last—the end. Until——

'Why did you go to Paris?' asks Nan, not through any overpowering desire to know, but because it is necessary to say something.

'Change. I wanted to get away somewhere. Dublin is a dull hole when all is told, and I thought a week in Paris would kill the cobwebs in my brain. Besides, Ferrars was there. You remember Ferrars?'

Nan nods her head. She doesn't remember Ferrars, but she is lost in a dream of her own at this moment, and it seems a happy arrangement of nature that a simple bow of the head should be as good as a spoken word.

'Well, he dropped me a line to join him, so I managed the leave and went. It was as dull there,' says Ffrench, in his disconsolate way. ' I couldn't see amusement in anything. Ferrars, too, seemed changed. After a week I came to a dead stick, and made up my mind to come back again—to come down here.'

He looks at her sideways to see how she takes this open hint—to find she has not been listening to him at all. There is an absent expression on her face not to be mistaken.

' I don't believe you heard one word of what I have been saying,' exclaims he wrathfully, his heavy brows meeting in a frown.

'Eh?' says Nan, startled. 'Oh yes. Yes, I assure you I heard everything. I quite agree with you.'

' That will do,' says he grimly.

'What do you mean? I really heard everything,' says Nan, rather shocked at her breach of manners, and still bent on being specially civil to him because of this last hopeless attachment of his.

'Did you? Come!' says he, with a disagreeable smile, 'what was the last word I said, eh?'

What, indeed! Nan looks up and Nan looks down; but heaven and earth seem to have forsaken her. What had he been talking about? Suddenly a vague memory, a single word or two, returning to that anxious inquirer, her brain, gives her hope.

'Why, of course,' she says brightly; 'just at first I couldn't remember quite the last words—one often feels puzzled about the simplest things when unexpectedly put to the test; but "dead stick" were the words, eh? I'm right, am I not? Yes, yes, I told you I agreed with you; they do rather spoil the general effect of the' (airily) 'exquisite green of the young spring shoots; but I suppose poor old Winter does not want to be forgotten all at once. He leaves us the dead branches here and there to remind us of his work. Though, after all,' plaintively this, 'I dare say it is age, not frost and snow, that kills so much of the underwood. What do you think ?'

'You leave me without thought,' says he, in a tone that makes her look at him.

'What a ridiculous answer,' returns she, 'and,' after a closer scrutiny of his frowning countenance, 'what an expression ! You must have some thought about it, you know.'

'About what ? What you have just said ?'

'Yes.'

'I think you are one of the most ingenious people I know. Will that do ?'

'Nonsense ! And all because I expressed a silly opinion about a dead stick ? I don't believe,' glancing at him sharply, 'that you have been attending to a word that I have said.'

At this, a low laugh breaks from Ffrench.

'I did you scant justice,' says he bitterly. 'In your own line you are inimitable. Here is your way to Rathmore, is it not ? Over this stile ?'

'You will not come on, then ?'

'Not now. I have an engagement.'

'Cold-hearted love,' says she, smiling, a little glad

at the thought that he may not suffer so very much in the long-run when Penelope refuses him. She is a little puzzled by the glance with which he receives this accusation. The reproach in it could be easily understood—why should she doubt his affection for Penelope ? But the something else in it, to which she can give no name—what did that mean ? what was it ?

It troubles her a little all the way to the house after she had bidden him good-bye, and is still in her mind when she enters the old schoolroom at Rathmore, where Murphy tells her she shall find Penelope.

CHAPTER VIII.

' I lived my life, I had my day,
  And now I feel it more and more.
The game I have no strength to play
  Seems better than it seemed of yore.'

HER first thought as she sees Penelope is how ill she is looking. The twilight is already gathering, and the schoolroom is dark save for the fire that burns brilliantly in the grate. Penelope, lying back in a dilapidated arm-chair that has seen much service and suffered many things at the hands of all the young Delaneys, starts into life as her sister enters, and runs to greet her, but even this quick flow of life fails to obliterate the knowledge that a moment ago she was leaning back, listless, tired, bloodless. Now, a little colour has sprung to her cheek, but it fades again, as the first excitement of Nan's unexpected coming is at an end and leaves her deadly pale.

She looks indeed as if she had received some sudden shock, or was suffering from an attack of nervous agitation. Nan, whose arm is round her, can feel that her heart is beating with an almost suffocating haste.

'Why, Penny, what is it?' says she; 'sit down, darling, and rest for a moment. How you started when I came in! It might have been a regular bogey you saw, instead of your own old Nan.'

'Nan!' says Penelope in a low tone, 'he is here! He is in the country! Did you know?'

'Yes,' says Nan. 'I met him just now—but surely that need not——'

'Met him; where?'

'In Hume wood. Close to the old stile.'

Penelope, who has leant forward in her eagerness, now sinks back in her chair again—a prey to despair. So near. At the door almost, and never to come in! Oh! when William told her this morning that Freddy Croker had come down, she had hoped, believed, prayed, that some time during the day he would come to her, and now—— The very bitterness of death seems to have touched her.

'What was he doing there?' she asks presently, when she has compelled herself to overcome the faintness that is threatening to conquer her.

'That's what I want to know,' says Nan irritably. 'He was always a gloomy sort of person; perhaps he thought he could gloom better in a lonely wood than anywhere else.'

'Not always. He used to be so different.'

'Used he? You must be the cause then of his deterioration of late. Ever since he fell in love with you, he has been in my opinion the most dismal person on record.'

Penelope, rising abruptly, pushes Nan's hands away and stands back from her with miserable offended eyes.

'I will have no jests on that subject,' she says in a choked voice. 'Think of me as you will, you cannot think more poorly of me than I think of myself; but —but—I will not have you speak of him in—in that way.'

'But why?' asks Nan aghast. 'I can see no harm in it. If he loves you——'

'He does not love me!' with a little fierce gesture.

' Well, he says he does : he said so just now ; and that he was coming to see you presently. I asked him what brought him back from Paris, and——'

' From Paris !' cries Penelope harshly. She stops, and gazes at Nan for awhile in dead silence, then lifting one hand covers her eyes with it. ' Oh ! of whom have you been speaking ?' she asks faintly.

' Why, of Boyle,' says Nan troubled. Terribly troubled now, for she has guessed the truth, and the cruelty of her own blunder. ' He—' with confusion. ' He—does love you, Penny.' She has laid her hand upon Penelope's shoulder, but the latter shakes her off.

' How dare you say that to me !' she says in a low tone, but vehemently. ' You—you of all others. This is the second time, Nan, and I warn you not to do it again. Are you a hypocrite ? Am I a fool ? Am I the only one, do you think, that can read between the lines ? Disguise it to yourself if you will —but in your heart you know that Boyle Ffrench still loves you, and you only.'

' Oh no, no !' cries Nan, shrinking back terrified. And then, forgetful of herself, of her own chagrin

and fear, of everything save her sister's deep unhappiness, she kneels down beside her, and encircles
her fondly with her arms. 'Penny!' whispers she
softly, her cheek against Penelope's, 'darling! If—
if it was not Boyle of whom you thought just now,
who was it?'

No answer, only Penelope so turns her head that
her lips come against Nan's cheek. Poor pretty lips,
cold and trembling.

'Speak to me. It will do you good. It was
Freddy, was it not? Oh! is it like that with you
still?'

'It will always be like that with me,' says Penelope.

She sighs heavily, and leans her head upon Nan's
shoulder as if tired out.

'It is killing me,' she says. 'I am dying of it. It
is silly, weak, anything you like, but I can't conquer
it. And it is all the more ridiculous because it never
really occurred to me that I liked him—in—in that
way, until I found he did not care for me.'

'Well, listen to me,' says Nan vehemently, who is
now crying. 'You are wrong, wrong. Freddy does
love you; I know it; I feel it. But, oh!' with an

angry sob, 'what a horrid fellow he is, not to come and say so !'

It is this identical moment that Mr. Murphy elects to throw open the door, and blink round him through the ever-increasing darkness.

'Are ye there, Miss Penelope?' says he. 'Misther Croker is in the drawin'-room, an' wants to see ye !'

Tableau.

'Where?' asks Nan at last, when she has assured herself, by pressing Penelope's hands, that she is all right, and not likely to go off in one of those weak fainting fits that have been annoying her of late. 'In the drawing-room, did you say, Murphy?'

'An' is that you, Miss Nan? Faith, I didn't see ye, me dear. Yes, miss—ma'am, I mane. I put him in there, an' a lamp along with him. He looked so down in the mouth, the crathure, that I thought the dark might disthress him. Fegs, be the look ov him, I'd say he was haunted. Musha! 'tis a hard life thim councillors have. For ivery boy they give to the rope, there's a ghost to follow thim iver after, so they say. Oh, murdher, miss! isn't that an awful thought? an' isn't it hard they earn their money?'

Good old Murphy! unconsciously he has given them time to recover themselves.

'Say Miss Penelope will be in presently,' says Nan calmly, and Murphy having returned with his message she turns to Penelope.

'Come, pull yourself together,' says she heartily, 'and pinch your cheeks a bit, to bring the colour into them.'

'It is only a formal visit,' says Penelope, looking hard at her, the anguish of a shamed confession later on bearing her to the earth. 'Don't think otherwise, Nan. Don't—I'—her voice falters—'I—shan't be able to bear it if you do.'

'Don't cry!' says the clever Nan quickly. 'I shan't think anything. Why, what are you thinking about, stupid? why shouldn't Freddy come and see us if he likes? There, don't keep him waiting; and give him my love, if either of you have time to think of me.'

She pushes Penelope gently out of the room as she speaks, and executes a little joyous *pas seul* on the threshold as she sees her disappear in the direction of the drawing-room.

CHAPTER IX.

'But she abideth silent, fair,
  All shaded by her flaxen hair,
    The blushes come and go ;
    I look, and I no more can speak—'

THE gaunt old room, with its scanty furniture, and faded walls and curtains, looks even more dejected than usual in the dim light emitted by the solitary lamp that Mr. Murphy had given to Croker as company. Penelope, entering by the lower door, seems indistinct and shadowy, and indeed it is only when his hand has closed over hers, that her visitor can see how altered she is. Not less lovely, perhaps, but too fragile—too ethereal. Her blue eyes seem almost too large for the pale small face, and dark rings lie beneath them ; the soft, sweet mouth has gained a little mournful curve, and the masses of fair hair that frame the forehead seem too heavy to be borne by the pensive face beneath.

'I hope I have not disturbed you,' says Croker in the most ordinary society tone, whilst his heart is sinking within him at the change in her. 'Murphy said someone was with you.'

'Only Nan, and she is going now. Won't you sit down ?'

A little troubled flame has crept into her white cheeks, owing to the fact that he is still holding her hand. He has forgotten that he holds it ; gazing at her, wondering, with a growing sense of misery, he has, indeed, forgotten everything, except that the one creature who on earth is dear to him, looks as though she were about to leave it.

'You have been ill,' he says abruptly.

The society tone has dropped out of use entirely.

'Oh no,' shaking her head. 'At least—it is nothing to signify. A cold ; the winter was severe, one cannot hope to escape everything.'

She breaks off confusedly.

'You, at least, have not been clever about it,' says he. 'You have escaped nothing, it seems to me.'

Then, with a frown, 'What are your people thinking about?' You should go somewhere for change of air.'

'One of my people agrees with you,' with a half-smile. 'Nan says she will take me to London with her, when she and her husband go there in May. But I don't care to go,' listlessly. 'I am quite well—quite strong, really. It is a mere passing weakness. There is no necessity for anyone to trouble about me.'

'I think there is—the greatest,' says Croker gravely. His tone, his whole air, is grave indeed, almost to severity. To Penelope it seems as if it is some stranger she is listening to, not an old, old friend. This subdued, embarrassed, serious person, who is he? where is the merry Freddy Croker of last summer? Alas! where are all the fond and tender girlish hopes that then bloomed and shed a fragrance round her life?

'You will go with her?' he asks presently.

'Yes; I suppose so.'

'You will enjoy a season in town.'

'I don't think so,' a little coldly.

After this there is a short silence, which Croker spends leaning forward in his chair, and gazing gloomily on the obliterated flowers of the carpet at his feet.

'I saw Boyle Ffrench just now,' says he at last, without looking up.

'Did you ? Nan met him too. We fancied him abroad, but it appears he returned last night.' There is an entire lack of interest in her manner.

' He—was coming from here, I suppose, when I met him ?' He asks this question with difficulty, and, indeed, despises himself as he does so. An uncontrollable longing to see her again has driven him back to the country with an undefined intention in his mind. At this moment he wishes he had never come. After battling with himself for three interminable months, he has given way—for what ? To find Ffrench just leaving her presence.

' From here ? No,' says Penelope's clear voice. ' I have not seen him.'

' You haven't ?' He lifts his eyes to hers at last, and a dull red darkens his brow.

' No,' indifferently. ' He told Nan, however, that

he was coming to see us before leaving. That will be to-morrow, I dare say.'

' Or this evening ?'

'Hardly now, I think,' glancing at the clock. ' But tell me about yourself,' with a gentle politeness ; 'you are getting on wonderfully, are you not ? We hear of you, you see, if not from you. It was such a surprise to us to learn you were once more in the country. Two surprises in one day are almost too much for dull people like us,' with a sweet but joyless smile. ' That you and Boyle should both come together was a trial to our nerves.' She pauses, and then she says simply, 'You have been a long time away.'

It is not intentional, but there is something so wistful in her voice that it should have touched him. Man-like, being occupied with his own one idea, he does not hear it.

' There was nothing to bring me here,' he says in a low tone, that it is pleasing to know arises out of the extreme misery he is enduring.

Penelope, with a swift movement, stoops and, taking up the poker, stirs the fire vigorously if with-

out discretion.   When she lifts her face again, though
white to the lips, she is quite tranquil.

' It would be folly to resent such a speech as that,'
she says prettily.   ' Though we, poor dwellers in the
dark corners of the earth, naturally dislike to hear
that there is no attraction in the spots where we
perforce must dwell.   Yes ; the country, lovely as it is,
must always give way to the town—in the winter,
specially.'

Her tone is quite calm.   She has even compelled
her sad lips to smile.   There was indeed one awful
moment when she thought she was going to cry,
but pride—that mighty deliverer—came to her aid
and supported her.

' As for that——' says Croker, beginning valiantly,
but failing all at once.   Whatever he was going to
say dies a sudden death, and the conversation
generally bids fair to follow its example.   Silence,
awful, unconquerable, threatens them.   The situation
is indeed becoming terrible, when Penelope flings
herself into the breach.

' As for what ?' she asks, with an attempt at the
charming gaiety that used to distinguish her.   Did

your conscience forbid you to say the polite thing? Come. Now you have confessed your horror of the "silent country," as somebody calls it, it is surely fair to ask you what has brought you here to-day.'

Croker hesitates. He raises his eyes suddenly, and fixes them on her, in a way that makes her long to shrink, and fade, and die away out of sight. What has she said?

'You!' says he shortly, at last.

A crimson flush dies Penelope's brow, a cruel burning flush that, fading presently, leaves her, if possible, paler than before. A last remnant of self-possession, clinging to her, induces her to throw up her shapely head and answer him as lightly as she can.

'You are happier, then, than most,' she says with a soft laugh; 'you have gained your desire. You see me.'

'And yet,' says he unsteadily, 'you are wrong when you call me happy, Penelope!' He rises and comes towards her with such uncontrollable agitation in his manner that involuntarily she rises too, and puts out both her hands as though to warn him from her.   Unkind little hands! He seizes them and holds them prisoners as his angry, despairing confession breaks from him.

'Against my will, my better judgment, I am here this evening,' he says passionately. 'With all my strength I fought against the coming, but you were too strong for me.   I could not keep away.   Much as I hate and despise myself for my weakness, I find that I must come to you—to tell you—that I love you.'

Penelope gently, but with determination, frees her hands.

'If it costs you so much——   Where is the necessity?' asks she, with a touch of hauteur, that mounts above even the thrill of rapture that rushes through her whole being.

'There is none.   I know that.   All the words you could say could not make that clearer to me.   But' —pushing back the short hair from his forehead—'I have told you.   That is something.   Perhaps after this I shall find peace of some sort.   It is all over now, Penelope, is it not?   All the old friendship—the past I used to so believe in—everything that makes life worth living. There is but one thing more to be done. Do it quickly, and let me go.'

'Do what?'

'Reject me! I have a strange fancy,' says he miserably, 'to hear you give me my dismissal.'

'Have you?' with ill-repressed wrath. 'A kindly fancy, I must say. And now supposing—merely supposing'—a pale smile wreathing her lips, whilst her eyes flash ominously—'that I don't reject you: what then?'

'This is unworthy of you,' says he in a low tone.

'How is it unworthy?' clasping her hands one over the other, as if to compel herself to be calm.

'If you cannot see it as I do, you must be greatly changed from the Penelope that once I thought I knew,' says he very unhappily.

'But why—why?' with almost ungovernable impatience.

'A girl who, loving one man, could listen to another, I——'

'What girl is that?' cries she, an angry sob quickening her voice. Croker looks keenly at her.

'Penelope,' says he sharply, 'are you engaged to Ffrench ?'

'To Boyle? No.'

'Can you,' with growing agitation, 'say honestly that there is nothing between you—that you do not—care for him !'

'Certainly I can,' her voice now vibrating with indignation. Undaunted by this, he takes her hands again, but she flings him from her, as if his touch hurts her.

'And so—and so,' she says, as if stifled, 'that was your thought! And for an idle, foolish fancy such as that you threw me off—without a word of explanation—without so much as troubling yourself to ask me : was it, or was it not so? You left me here alone all these weary months to think just as I would of you. You speak of love ; but if you had truly loved me, would not my good opinion have been of all things the most necessary to you? Oh no,' seeing him about to speak, 'not a word. I will not hear. Oh, all that I have suffered ! No excuses—nothing could kill the memory of the past.'

'You cannot forgive, then ? Penelope, there are

some things that I think you should remember, if only in common fairness to me.'

' I don't know what those things may be ; there are long hours and days of cruel wondering that have blotted them out. No, no, go your way, and let me go mine. It is impossible that I should forget; you spoke of old days, past friendship: surely it is I— who——'

She breaks off suddenly, and bursts into a storm of weeping that shakes all her fragile frame.

' Go !' she says, pointing with one hand to the door.

' You will not pardon me, then,' says he with poignant anguish, hesitating to obey a command that will part him from her for ever.

No answer.

Slowly he moves towards the door ; yes, as he had himself said, it is all over. Bewildered, stunned by the discovery that, after all, he had misjudged her, that she was free for him to win—nay more, that she was already won by him—he pushes aside a chair on his slow march down the room, scarcely knowing where he is going. His kindly, honest face is a very triumph of despair ; his brain is in a whirl. What on earth is to become of him !

Here his hand finding the handle of the door, he looks back once more—for the last time, as he tells himself.

'Good-bye, Penelope !' says he slowly, in a voice that might have melted an iceberg.

'Good-bye,' returns she, in a tone hardly audible from behind her handkerchief.

Again his fingers close upon the handle of the door, which rattles ominously.

'Try to think kindly of me sometimes—if, indeed, you can care to think of me at all,' says he, out of the depths of an unfathomable gloom. He draws the door slowly towards him.

'Oh !' cries Penelope in a terrible way. She flings her handkerchief upon the ground, and looks at him. 'Where are you going ?' sobs she, with considerably more indignation than tenderness. 'What do you mean by it all ? Oh !' with withering emphasis. 'To think that you should be so hateful to me !'

'But, Penelope——' begins the unfortunate lover. He finds himself at her side again, almost before he has had time to think about it ; and a little more absent-mindedness suffices to place his arms round her. Penelope, who is still crying, but now with the greatest enjoyment, forgets to rebuke him, even when she wakes to the fact that he is kissing her with a very decided warmth.

'You don't deserve it,' says she irrelevantly, lifting her pretty drenched eyes to his. She makes a futile effort to push him from her.

'I know it—but—Penny, you know how I love you !'

'No I don't,' says she wrathfully. And then all at once capitulating, she lays her head upon his breast, and clings to him with an honest, loving fervour. 'Freddy,' whispers she with strong reproach, 'why did you not say that sooner ?'

'I was mad, I think,' says he with a groan that is all self-contempt. 'Darling ! darling heart ! forget it, if you can.'

'Well—I'll try,' says she with a truly soulrending sigh.

CHAPTER X.

' Answered a little bird overhead,
  As birds will do in summer ;
"Somebody has kept tryst," it said,
"With somebody else in a kirtle red,
And they are going to be married :"
  Sing heigh, sing ho, for the summer !'

PRESENTLY, lifting her head, she looks at him.

'I thought you were in love with some horrid girl in Dublin,' she says, gazing anxiously at him, as though still some doubt born of that cruel suspicion is with her.

'Then you doubted me, too!' says he joyfully. 'If you confess to that, you should let me off easily. Oh, Penelope, I think your crime greater than mine, for you must have known that in the whole wide world there is no one who could be compared with you, whereas, so far as I am concerned, you might find at every corner just such a one as myself.'

'Indeed I could not,' says Penelope vehemently. 'Freddy! I think that girl in Dublin was killing me.'

'But there wasn't any girl,' says Croker.

'Never mind ; there might have been.'

'There might not,' with determination. 'I must say, Penelope, I call this most unfair. How can you love me, and yet——'

'Oh, I do, I do !' cries Penelope, pressing her cheek against his. 'It is only that I can't help fancying that everyone who saw you must have loved you, too.'

She makes this remarkable declaration quite boldly, and as she says it looks at him quite bravely, as though defying anyone to see cause for laughter in it. Perhaps she herself sees none. She is indeed apparently without shame at the thought that she has committed herself to a good deal, and that it might be that others might not consider Croker so born an Adonis as she does. That both she and Croker think each other perfection is plain to see.

The Mutual Admiration Society has in them as ardent a couple of members as need be desired.

It is perhaps fortunate that just at this moment Gladys enters the room.

' It is only just now that Murphy told me you were here,' she says, addressing Croker with that slight air of constraint that has marked all their dealings with him of late. ' It appears Nan was here too, and no one sent me word,' with an injured glance at Penelope. ' How d'ye do ?' holding out her hand to Croker, whereupon he—whose heart is overflowing with loving-kindness towards all the world—promptly lays his arm around her neck and gives her a most affectionate kiss. ' Freddy ! Freddy ! are you mad !' cries she, shaking him off and staring at him with crimson cheeks. ' Well, really, Freddy ! Upon my word ! This is—I must say—a little too much ! Are these Dublin manners, I wonder ?' demands the irate little thing, drawing herself up until she looks quite tall, and ' of age.' ' If so, I don't care about them. Have you been as lavish of your attentions to Penelope ?' Here she pauses to look at her sister, after which she turns her look into a stare.

'Penelope, what's the matter with you?' demands she.

'The matter?' repeats Penelope feebly, who, indeed, is beginning to feel distinctly ashamed of herself.

'Yes—the matter,' unflinchingly. 'I left you an hour ago as pale as a marble statue ; I find you now looking as disgracefully robust as the orthodox milk-maid. Freddy, have you been painting her cheeks?'

No answer from Freddy, no answer from Penelope : like two culprits they stand looking from east to west, but gaining inspiration from neither quarter. Things are growing serious, when at last, as Penelope once more hopelessly turns her head eastwards, light dawns upon Gladys (coming presumably from that awakening spot), and suddenly her severity vanishes, and smiles and embryo congratulations take its place.

'Why,' says she, dimpling, and spreading out her hands, 'is it? Eh? Oh, I am glad! Oh, Freddy, was that why you kissed me? Come here, come here at once, and do it all over again.'

Freddy does it all over again, and has no reason to complain of his reception this time.

'It's the most delightful thing,' says Gladys, who
is as pleased as though she were herself the one to be
congratulated. 'So different from poor darling Nan's
affair, because you two are in love. So nice! I like
a real romance when one can get it. Why, Freddy,
you'll be my brother!' as if rather wondering at this
strange fact.

'Yes,' says Croker, who is sitting beside Penelope
now, with her fingers tightly squeezed up within his
own. He is almost afraid to be as happy as he feels.
The Irish blood running now so warmly within his
veins is so far charged with the superstition that
marks the race—peer and peasant alike—that he
shrinks a little from the rapture that in spite of him
is flooding all his veins. 'I hope I shall be a good
brother,' says he.

'I hope I shall be a good sister. I'm not good to
William,' says Gladys, with a determination to be
honest at all costs. 'Sometimes I really feel that I
can't bear William. He's so presumptuous! Only
yesterday he told me that he knew a great deal more
about the rearing of fowls than I do—I, who spend
my life at it! But never mind,' says she, flinging

aside her sudden attack of anger, her breeding telling her it is no fit food for glad young lovers such as these, ' William isn't all the world !' This undeniable fact she lays bare to them with a pretty nod, and throwing out fresh dimples with a view to letting them see how thoroughly in accord she is with them in their new-found happiness, she goes on, smiling at Croker, 'You won't tell me I never heard of the "pip," will you ?'

'The pip?' questions Croker uncertainly, and feeling horribly sorry that his general ignorance should at this particular moment be made so distinctly apparent.

'It is a disease that the chickens sometimes have,' explains Penelope softly.

'Oh yes ; I see. Well,' looking at Gladys, 'it is plain that I can't question your knowledge. As for William, I feel sure his ignorance is astounding ; he ought to be ashamed of himself.'

'He isn't,' says Gladys plaintively. ' He thinks I know nothing. But,' beaming upon the lovers, 'what does anything signify besides this delightful news ! Does Nan know?'

'Oh, I never thought of Nan,' says Penelope, starting. 'She said something about going home when I left her to come here to Freddy,' with a rapturous glance at the happy Croker and a warm pressure of her hand. 'But if she should be in the schoolroom all this time, waiting for me! Oh, poor Nan!'

Simultaneously, filled with pity for the neglected Nan, they all rush to the schoolroom—to find their pity thrown away. Nan is no longer there.

CHAPTER XI.

' The winter wind is not so cold
As the bright smile he sees me win.'

NAN, indeed, tired of waiting, and finding the daylight waning with alarming haste, had decided on taking her homeward way without any further waste of time, leaving the morrow to bring her word of what had transpired at Croker's visit to Penelope.

Stepping into the open air, she finds that already twilight is giving place to night, and not being above those qualms of fear that sometimes attend the nervous wanderer in darksome places, it is with a distinctly frightened face she mounts the stile and drops into the woods at Hume. A mental determination never to spend the afternoon again at Rathmore during the short spring days without giving orders for the carriage to call for her and take her home

suggests itself to her as she steps lightly over the
brawling brook that seems to roar with fierce threat-
enings in the silence of the gloomy trees.

> ' The dark, delicious, dreamy forest way,
>   The hope of April for the soul of May ;
> On all of these Night's wide soft wings swept down.'

Sweet to her as all this might be in broad sunshine,
to-night it fills her with naught but an absurd terror
that increases ever as she goes, though every now and
then, as she forgets her fears, the serene and perfect
beauty of the evening makes itself felt, and steals
upon her heart.   To quote once again from Mr.
Nesbit's charming poem :

> ' One yellow star pierced through the clear, pure sky,
>   And showed above the network of the wood,
>   The silence of whose crowded solitude
>   Was broken but by little woodland things,
>   Rustling dead leaves with restless feet and wings,
>   And by a kiss that ended in a sigh.'

She has almost lost herself in the pleasure of these
joys of nature, when a sound behind her renews all
her fears.   Steps, unmistakable footsteps.   How
dreadfully dark it is, and how far from Hume !

Turning abruptly, as if safety lies in facing the foe, she finds herself looking at Boyle Ffrench.

'You again !' she says, with an austerity born partly of her late unreasoning terror, and partly of an anger that has been growing unconsciously, and is now a prodigious size. 'Have you lost your way? You must turn right round if you want to go to Rathmore.'

' I am afraid it is too late to go there now,' says he uneasily ; ' Julia was especially annoying this afternoon : she kept me until I felt I could hardly call at Rathmore without comment.'

'Why should you fear comment ?' says she, with a frown that escapes him in the dark. It is a little unkind of her, if one considers her hopes about Freddy ; but a doubt of Boyle's sincerity, lately come to her, has at this moment started into full life.

' I fear nothing,' says he calmly, a sudden fancy taking him that she is taunting him with his studied coldness towards herself. ' Don't mistake me there. I would dare all that man can if I was sure that——'

' You mustn't be too sure,' says Nan hastily, frightened, when she thinks that even now at this moment

all things may be right between Penelope and Croker.
'You must wait.   There may be failure even at the
last.'

'Not when there is mutual love—and courage with
it,' says he warily, trying to pierce her expression in
the growing gloom, and failing.

'I dare say there may be something in that,' says
she indifferently, hardly knowing what to say.   'Well,
and you left poor Julia ?'

'Yes.   She was unbearable.   She deals in so many
innuendoes of late that one can scarcely follow her.
At all events, to attempt it is to be wearied beyond
bearing.   I thought that perhaps you would not mind
if I came up to Hume a little early, and so I ordered
my clothes to be sent after me.'

When first he came up with her he had spoken
breathlessly, as one might who has been running.   A
quick fancy that he had been lying in wait for her,
and had hurried after her, touching her mind, had
raised within her a sense of injury hardly to be
allayed.   It is, therefore, with the very barest
courtesy that she now answers him.

'We shall be glad to see you at any time,' she

says icily, taking comfort from that 'we.' Then presently, 'How have you offended Julia ?'

'You know her as well as I do; you can understand how easy it is to offend Julia,' replies he evasively. 'Give her the barest inch of an idea, and she turns it into an ell. Are you going home now ? May I walk with you ?'

'Yes,' very coldly ; those words of Penelope now cry loudly to her. Was there truth in them ? 'You can come,' she says ; 'though I confess I had calculated on having the pleasure of a walk all by myself.' This is not only distinctly untrue (as there had been no pleasure in the idea of the solitary walk before her), but extremely uncivil, and Ffrench, whose hopes had risen high, cools before it.

'Don't let me spoil your pleasure,' says he suddenly. 'I can quite understand the charm that solitude presents to most people. I myself know it. That path there,' pointing to one on his right, 'leads to the garden, I think ; if I take it, I shall be at Hume almost as soon as you.'

'Ye-es,' says Nan faintly. Her heart fails her as she thinks of the long lonely walk that lies between

her and home. Disagreeable as Boyle's company
may be, it is surely better than none under the circumstances. As she hesitates, hardly knowing what
to do, the sound of a gun close at hand startles her,
and brings a quick colour to her cheeks.

'That must be George,' says she hurriedly, and
Ffrench, noting the haste and the sudden flush, comes
to the conclusion that best pleases him : she had
evidently known that Hume was shooting this wood,
and that therefore at any moment she might meet
with him. Hence her anxiety to get rid of him (Boyle).

'George !' calls Nan. 'George !' Her clear young
voice rings lightly through the air, and at length
reaches Hume, who had been shooting all the afternoon, and had now sent a last desultory shot—useless because of the dead daylight—after a dissipated
young rabbit who should have been abed an hour
agone.

'Here I am,' says he, dropping over a low wall
and coming towards her. There is a smile upon his
face. So seldom has his Christian name been spoken
by her, that the sound of it coming from her lips is as
music to him.

The smile disappears, however, and his brow clouds a little, as he sees her companion. Clouds, but clears again directly, leaving, however, a certain gravity behind—a sort of compromise, as it were, between the two expressions.

'Boyle is coming up to dinner,' says Nan.

'How d'ye do? Didn't know you were in this part of the world,' says Hume, shaking hands with Ffrench.

'Came down this morning,' says Ffrench indifferently.

'Had good sport?' asks Nan, turning to her husband, and, to his everlasting amazement, tucking her arm quite confidentially into his. Truly, she is a woman of many moods—impossible to understand. Only this morning she had treated Hume to a very considerable show of temper, all about nothing really when he came to look into it. She had given him what she was pleased to call a piece of her mind, though he had had so many pieces already that he might reasonably be supposed by this time to be in possession of the whole of it. Finally, she had left him, with a declaration to the effect that in her opinion he was one of the poorest creatures it had ever been her misfortune to meet; and here she is now smuggling her little pretty hand through the arm of the poorest creature, and apparently on the very best of terms with him. It occurs to Hume, in a half-amused puzzlement, that a few more of these startling alterations and his brain will give way.

Meantime, Nan is chatting gaily, brightly, glancing a little defiantly as she does so at Ffrench over her husband's shoulder. The woodland path is narrow, and Ffrench is constrained, therefore, to walk behind them. A sensation of relief, of protection, has raised Nan's mercurial temperament to the seventh heavens, and she is now as happy as though there is no smallest thing in all her life to trouble her.

This frame of mind supports her through all the evening. It helps her even to the selection of a gown that makes her a very vision of beauty when she sweeps down to dinner to dazzle the eyes of the two men who love her.

There is a slight touch of coldness, of suspicion, in her manner towards Ffrench, that inflames the unhappy passion that is demoralizing him, and kills the last germs of good in a character not at any time finely wrought.

Something in his whole air and bearing to-night, in a subtle, unaccountable way, so far offends Nan that her beauty, towards the close of the night, grows imperious, and it is with reluctant fingers and a cold, smileless face she accepts his adieux. Yet she could hardly have explained to herself where the offence lay, and, when he is gone, stands tapping dreamily upon a quaint little table at her elbow, trying vainly to arrange and fix her accusation. Is it all imagination, born of Penelope's warning, or—that old story —did it still live?

The thought is intolerable. The very suspicion of it angers her almost beyond endurance. She had believed him when he spoke of—or had implied, rather—his love for Penelope. If he had lied to her in that instance, making use of her own sister to shield from her his guilty affection for herself, he was base above his fellows. The impatient taps upon the table grow louder, and at last, as if unable to bear her thoughts in silence any longer, the words break from her.

'If—if that is true, he has been insufferably imper-tinent !' says she aloud, her supple figure growing rigid, in an angry haughtiness.

'Has he?' says Hume calmly. He had entered the room without her hearing him, and now, leaning against the piano, looks at her over the top of it.

CHAPTER XII.

'His sweetest friend or hardest foe,
    Best angel or worse devil;
I either hate or love him so,
    I can't be merely civil.'

*   *   *   *   *

NAN starts violently. Ceasing the impatient drumming, she looks round at him, a disturbed, angry,
lovely creature. Her white gown rustles as though
a nervous trembling had run through all her limbs,
and the pearls round her throat rise and fall with
the heaving of her bosom. She had been lost in
unpleasant speculation, and this sudden coming back
to everyday topics has both alarmed and annoyed
her. Honestly, too, it takes but a little thing at any
time to raise within her breast an antagonistic feeling
towards Hume.

The latter gazes at her with mingled emotions, passionate longing, settled despair. Of late it has seemed to him that to hope still longer is but to give place to folly. She will never care for him. Her strange friendliness of the afternoon had not deceived him one whit. He is tired of her caprices by this time. And, perhaps, coquette as she is to her heart's core, it was but with a view to enraging Ffrench that she had thus slipped her arm within his—Hume's —and chatted to him with that pretty enforced gaiety.

He had been civility itself to Ffrench all the evening. He took, indeed, a special pleasure at all times in showering upon him every courtesy within his power. It was inevitable that he should feel a contempt for the man, who, whilst knowing himself in love with the wife, was still equal to accepting hospitality from the husband, and mixed, therefore, with the unvarying politeness he ever showed him, there was a large pinch of malevolence, impossible to subdue. To press courtesies upon Ffrench, and see him accept them, gave him a sense of bitter enjoyment the extent of which could only be measured by the amount of baseness betrayed by the recipient of them. To sit face to face with Ffrench, and know him to be a traitor, gave him a sense of moral superiority that was soothing—a paltry kind of vengeance, no doubt, but we are all human.

He had purposely kept aloof from the drawing-room to-night. It was a sort of wounding pleasure to himself to know that he did not interfere with the fellow at all—that he could give him freely to understand that he feared him in nowise. On the stroke of eleven he had strolled into the room where Ffrench and his wife sat, to beg the former to stay a little longer when he rose to depart. He had followed him into the hall, to press upon him one of his choicest cigars ; and if he had not been able entirely to control the superciliousness that marked his tone, Ffrench, at least, had not seemed to notice it.

He was not in the habit of returning to the drawing-room once his guests had departed, but to-night a sudden longing to see Nan again had induced him to do so ; yet now as he watches her beautiful face turned upon him with petulance, a wish that he had taken his usual way to the smoking-room instead is strong upon him. His face is quite calm, however, as he returns her gaze steadily, and a desire to learn the meaning of her words keeps him where he is.

'How you startled me!' says Nan with a frown. 'What a habit that is, entering a room without giving a sign of your coming! I really wish you would cure yourself of such horrid ways.'

'I am afraid you must blame your thoughts, not me. They were evidently engrossing,' says he slowly. Nan, with a shrug of her shoulders, goes over to the fire, and, sinking into an armchair, leans forward, her elbow on her knee, her chin in her hand. Hume, remaining standing by the piano, lets one finger travel slowly, mechanically, over the light shade of dust that the evening has laid upon the top of it. Mechanically, after a bit the finger forms a word, 'Impertinent.'

'And to her,' says he to himself, drawing his breath sharply.

Straightening himself and going up to the fire, he leans his back against the mantelpiece and looks down at her.

'Did Ffrench annoy you?' asks he bluntly.

The hot blood mounts to her forehead, but she shrugs her shoulders as before.

'I never let anyone annoy me,' says she coldly. 'Except you. I can't help you, of course.'

'I am afraid I must continue to annoy you for a few minutes. If he didn't annoy you, why did you call him impertinent awhile since?'

'Now, once for all,' says Nan, sitting up, 'I'm not going to be put into a microscope for you to examine at your leisure. I decline to be cross-questioned. If I happened to let fall that word "impertinent," who shall say it was applied to Boyle?'

'You are growing as ingenious as himself,' says he, with a slight sneer.

'Well, supposing it was about Boyle,' says she angrily, 'what then? I was only thinking that if he did so-and-so he was behaving abominably. No more than that. I have yet to prove that he did so behave.'

'You will not tell me, then, what it was all about?' shifting his position as if to leave her.

'Oh, if you must know!' cries she, shutting up her

fan with a vehement little snap, 'stay and hear it, He told me this morning—or, at all events, gave me to understand—that he had set his affections on Penelope, and to-night—somehow—I saw cause to doubt the truth of what he said.'

'And the cause ?'

'You are insatiable,' retorts she with a vexed laugh. 'But, here, I cannot answer you, simply because I can't answer myself. It was a mere impression.'

'Do you really find enjoyment in this sort of thing, Nan?' asks he gravely, laying his hand upon her shoulder. 'I hardly think it. And I fear it will bring you trouble some day. I know it is useless my speaking to you, but——'

'The whole thing is useless !' cries Nan, throwing out her hands with a gesture of despair. 'I suppose that you still think I am encouraging Boyle in a folly dead six months ago, if it ever lived ; and it is vain for me to assure you that you judge me falsely. Oh, bother Boyle !' cries she, suddenly springing to her feet. 'I wish, with all my heart, that I had never seen him.'

'You needn't see him any more,' says Hume slowly.

'If you think that, you don't know him.'

'If you think I couldn't prevent it, you don't know me,' calmly.

'Well, I won't have anything unkind said or done. He is unhappy enough as it is—so entirely dependent upon Julia, who is just like a weathercock. And if he is in love with Penelope, why, he hasn't a chance there.'

'And in the meantime you are letting people gossip about you. You,' with meaning, 'who so shrink from gossip.'

She turns slowly from him, until only her profile can be seen. Watching her rather anxiously now, he knows that she has grown very white.

'Don't remind me of that time—don't!' she says in a voice hardly above a whisper.

'I beg your pardon,' says Hume hastily. 'I had no idea that—— I am sorry you look back upon it all in that way.'

'Never mind,' says she, with a sweeping gesture of her hand, as though declining to discuss it. 'As a

fact, I never look back upon it. The memory is too
hateful. And as to gossip associating itself with my
name in this case,' flashing round at him, 'I don't
believe it. You, and you alone, seek to make mischief
out of it.'

'That's unfair. Besides, I am not the only one
who has argued the matter with you—hopelessly,
certainly. Your aunt, Mrs. Manly, has spoken to you,
I think.'

'Julia! Oh, Julia is a fool!' says Nan, reseating
herself, and throwing herself back in her chair, as if
argument has come to an end. 'She says now that
your conduct towards me was delightfully romantic.'

Something in the disgust of her tone, something in
the thought of Mrs. Manly advocating his cause,
strikes Hume as comic, and, in spite of himself, he
bursts out laughing.

'Does she? By Jove!' says he, 'I'm inclined
to think I haven't done justice to Julia. I owe
her something for that. I wonder what she would
like.'

'Like?' rousing herself to sit up and stare at
him.

'What sort of a present, I mean,' says he.

'You shan't give Julia a present,' says Nan, now effectually interested. 'I won't have it.'

'Why?' coldly.

'She's the very worst friend I have. She does nothing but say unkind things of me to the girls, and to you. No, no; you shall not flatter her like that.'

'I don't see how you can expect to control my actions,' says Hume icily. 'I shall certainly do as I choose in this matter. Why should I not make your aunt a present? I am going up to Cork to-morrow, and I shall look out for something that will please her.'

'To Cork to-morrow. Are you really going up to-morrow? I'll go too,' cries Nan, with avidity, for-getting her grievances in this new thought. 'I'm tired of being here. A change will be delightful.'

'Quite out of the question,' coldly.

'What is out of the question?' turning eyes full of the most intense astonishment on him. When before did he say no to a request of hers?

'Your coming with me to town to-morrow. I am

going strictly on business, and could not possibly pay any attention to you.'

' I shouldn't want you to,' says Mrs. Hume promptly.

' I dare say not,' grimly. ' But I don't see how you could get about by yourself. You know nothing of Cork. Besides, I shall just run up by the 9.40 train, and come down again by the 3.15. You'd be fagged to death and gain nothing by it.'

' I should gain a few hours' escape out of this dull place, at all events ; and, besides,' struck by a sudden happy thought, ' why come home by the afternoon train ? Why not stay there ? I want to go to the theatre. Toole is there now, playing " The Don." I feel as if I must see him. You could '—with a touch of cajolery, mixed with a pout—' take me if you liked.'

' Well,' unmoved by this attempt at corruption, and wisely refusing to look at her, ' say I don't like, then.'

' Do you mean to tell me you don't want to take me ?' demands Mrs. Hume, sitting bolt upright this time, as if to examine his features more closely, and make sure that she had heard him aright. Good heavens! Is it possible her ears have not deceived her?

'Oh, nonsense!' says Hume impatiently. And then—'I couldn't stay there for the night. It is specially important that I should get back here as soon as possible. I have told Harley to meet me here to-morrow night. If you troubled yourself to think of anything, you would understand that those leases must be looked into without delay. It will put me out extremely if you persist in this foolish fancy.'

'Very well; I don't care. I shall persist,' says she, with a mutinous glance at him from under her long lashes, that only makes her look like a naughty child.

He looks at her with deep sadness. If only she loved him, how easy it would be to fold her in his arms, and kiss away that rebellious little frown from her brow, and the wrath from out of her eyes.

'If I am persistent,' says she, 'and—a trouble to you, thank yourself for it. You married me in spite of me; it isn't my fault that I am your wife;

and now you have me I am going to make myself as
troublesome as ever I possibly can.'

'That threat loses its force,' says he, 'when I
call to mind your conduct ever since I married you.'
It is perhaps the bitterest thing he has ever said to
her.

A sudden silence seems to have caught and held
her. She looks at him with a very strange expression, and at last rises to her feet.

'Are you sorry you married me?' asks she, not
angrily or mournfully, but in a tone he has never
heard her use before.

'Yes,' returns he stormily, all his passion and
grief and despair breaking forth at last, 'unfeignedly
sorry. I would to heaven I had never seen you!
Each moment of my life is a separate misery because
of you. Do you think I am made of stone? that I
have no feeling? I have ruined your life and my
own. If you want revenge, you have it now in that
confession.'

He moves abruptly by her as if to leave the room.

'Stay one moment,' says she quickly, and he
pauses to look back at her. She is a little pale, but

neither angry nor aggrieved. There is only that new great wonder in her eyes. ' About to-morrow,' she says : ' I will not go with you. I will spare you a few miserable moments, at all events. You shall have one long happy day all to yourself !'

CHAPTER XIII.

'Was it touch of human passion
Made you woman in a fashion,
Beauty Clare?'

SHE is as good as her word. She puts in no appearance at breakfast next morning, and when Hume returns from Cork, after consulting his solicitor, it is to find she has gone to Rathmore, and has left a message to the effect that she will not be back ('home' is a word she persistently refuses to use in connection with the Castle) until the following day.

Hume, stricken with remorse, spends a terrible evening. All day long, indeed, he has been haunted by fears of what his impulsive words might have done. She would be certain to resent them, but how? The very uncertainty that clouds the answer to this momentous question enlarges the fear of it, and renders him doubly unhappy. He should not have spoken to her like that ; and yet, when he said he regretted his marriage with her, his thoughts were for her more than for himself. Surely he had ruined her life.

One little gleam of sunshine stood to him all through. If she had not wanted to marry him, surely she had not wanted to marry any other. He was as certain as he was of an hereafter that she cared in no smallest degree for Ffrench. On this thought he dwelt, as though in it alone lay salvation from the fears and difficulties that surrounded him—though not for a moment did he delude himself into the belief that she yet might care for him. Too much time had been given for that, and there was no result.

'No! I am not the fellow to suit her,' he tells himself despondingly now, as he paces up and down his library, the morning after his return from Cork, wondering anxiously when she will return. Supposing she should not return at all! His heart almost ceases to beat as this idea comes to him.

Had that single message of hers, saying that she

was going to sleep at Rathmore, meant more than on the outer surface appeared? Was it but a preliminary to a more decisive step? She had no love for him that he knew, and his last words to her might have roused within her a desire--a longing—to place between him and her a barrier that he might not overstep. Supposing she were never to return, that she should demand from him a separation ! He stands still, as one might who is stunned, and tries to compel himself to think this out.

And as he so stands, a sound comes to him of laughter and running steps and merry words, all mingled into one joyous whole. The door is burst open, and Nan, her face alight with mirth and mischief, and a delightful pretence at terror, rushes into the room, closely pursued by Bartle.

She glances wildly round her, sees Hume, and without a second's hesitation flies to him, and literally flings herself into his arms.

' Save me ! save me !' cries she in little broken breaths of laughter, clinging to him with both her arms.

Her lovely face is close to his, he can hear her

heart beat against his own, yet she never looks at him ; her whole mirthful soul is bent on the thought that she has triumphed over her pursuer.

'Pah!' says she impertinently, making a pretty grimace at Bartle over her husband's shoulder.

'Well, I call that beastly mean,' says Bartle, who has not yet quite ceased to be a boy. 'First you take advantage of its being April Fools' Day to insult me, and then you fly from a just vengeance, and having found a secure shelter, you turn and insult me again. I put it to you, Hume, is that decent behaviour ?'

But Hume finds no words in which to answer him. All at once his soul seems to have risen in revolt against the thoughtless cruelty of this one woman on whom its hopes are set. It is at an end now—

'All the hope and the fear and the sorrow.'

He will finish with it once for all, and put a period to his misery.

A very agony of regret for his own remorse of last night and this morning makes him tighten his grasp upon the slender creature resting so tranquilly, with so little emotion, within his grasp. He had cared so dreadfully, had so fretted himself for the pain that he believed she was enduring, and she—she had not cared at all.

He was so little to her that an unkind word from him had no smallest power to sting her. During all these past hours, when he was eating his heart out lest he should have hopelessly offended her, she had given no thought to him—had been one of the gayest in that merry home circle, to which she clung with an affection absorbing, complete, and from which she jealously excluded him.

The very *insouciance* of her manner to him, the lightness with which she had just now thrown herself into his embrace, proved more than all that had gone before that he was less than nothing to her.

He was a means of escape from Bartle, he gave her a chance of triumphing over that determined pursuer, that was all! She regarded him as she might a friendly wall behind which she could safely hide herself. Anybody else would have done quite as well.

The red flush that had mounted to his brow when first she had precipitated herself upon him, like a fragrant whirlwind has died now. He looks altogether very much as usual in spite of the angry heart-throbs, and the raging sense of injustice, that are consuming him.

'Pouf! a fig for you!' cries Nan airily, nodding at her brother. 'Mean? Who is mean? Except the man (save the mark!') — this with outrageous insolence—'who taunts a weak woman, and threatens her with instant death, all because she pinned a little memorandum to the tail of his coat — a memorandum consecrated to his many virtues!'

Here she goes off into a delicious peal of laughter. Evidently that memorandum had not been altogether complimentary.

'If I had caught you in the avenue,' begins Bartle, who is now roaring with laughter, too, 'I'd have——'

'Finished me?' audaciously. 'Well, you didn't —you couldn't. You aren't good enough.' She is still clinging to Hume, but now she turns as if to face Bartle more comfortably, and stands leaning her young *svelte* figure against her husband's shoulder. 'Why,' cries she defiantly, did you really think you could overtake me ? You overrate yourself, my good boy !' with a charming pout. 'Do you know,' looking up suddenly at her husband, with a lovely smile, 'he hunted me all the way from Rathmore to this house, and I had only four minutes' start of him, yet he could not catch me ! A poor creature I call him !'

'Try it back again,' says Bartle courageously.

'Tut, sir, bethink you ! Why, you are in the presence of a second Atalanta. I'd enter the lists with you, and such as you, without a tremor.'

'You tremored very considerably when you got to the library door,' says Bartle, flinging his taunt with joy. Nan laughs.

'Ah ! but I felt caged then, and I did not know he had come back from Cork. He might have stayed one more night. There was no longer an opening for me ; this room to which I foolishly had run was a mere *cul de sac*—how was I to escape ? But the gods stood to me,' cries she piously, and once again she looks up at Hume. 'How lovely of you to be here just the one only time in all my life that I wanted you,' says she with quite a brilliant touch of torture.

Still Hume says nothing. Will she ever go? Will it ever suggest itself to her to leave his arms and stand, or sit, or walk, or dance somewhere else?

'You never knew such a gay old time as we had at Rathmore last night,' she goes on, laughing now again as merrily as music can. 'We played "hide and seek" all over the house, until father arose in his wrath and condemned us all to solitary confinement for a month, whereon we—— Why, what's the matter with you?' says she, drawing back from him a little—the better to read his face. 'Are you ill?'

'No,' says Hume, speaking with an effort. Will she never go? Unconsciously he pushes her from him, but so gently that she hardly guesses the meaning of his action. It is an indescribable relief to him to put her in this way from him. If he could thus easily separate her life from his for ever and ever, how much better it would be. Great Heaven, that he should have come to think like this!

As she stands apart from him, he breathes more freely, and makes an unconscious movement with his arms that speaks of freedom gained.

'Well—you look it,' says Nan slowly, and this time with anxiety. 'You are as white as——'

'My looks belie me then,' says he curtly. 'I am perfectly well.'

'Perhaps you are sorry to see me back again,' says she, with a rather awkward little smile; like a lightning flash their late parting returns to her, and the red blood rushes to her brow. Until now she had hardly expended a thought on it, but something in his face quickens her imagination.

'Perhaps I am,' returns he bitterly.

Bartle, who is outside all this, takes it as jest, and gives Nan's arm a friendly pinch.

'One in the eye for you,' says he, with a chuckle. 'I am avenged! A thousand thanks, Hume, and farewell. Duty calls me!' At the door he looks back, gives up tragedy and returns to sanity. 'Keep that up, George,' says he maliciously. 'It will do her a world of good; bring her down a peg or two. She wants it. She's so conceited now, that no decent citizen can come within a mile or two of her.'

Having dexterously avoided the cushion Nan has sent flying at his head, he closes the door, and is heard presently singing down the hall. His footsteps grow less and less, and now are gone, and the two left standing in the library grow embarrassed over a silence that threatens to be everlasting.

Nan, being the woman, is of course the one to break it.

'You are angry,' says she plaintively, glancing at him sideways, in a half uncertain fashion. 'You are angry with me still, after all this time !'

Angry with her ! He had believed her angry with him. It was of so little consequence to her that she has already forgotten the rights of the case.

' I was never angry,' says he coldly.

'No ? Really ?' as if relieved certainly, but still in doubt. ' You are sure ?'

'Quite !' more coldly still.

' That's all right then,' says Nan, seating herself with all the air of one eager to begin a long and

exhaustive examination. 'Come, sit down and tell
me all about your visit to Cork. Did you enjoy
yourself? Did you see anyone? Were the shops
nice? Did you bring me anything?'

'No,' shortly.

A pause.

'Nothing at all?'

'Nothing.'

Longer pause.

'I hope,' with sudden suspicion, and peering into
his face, 'you didn't bring Julia anything?'

'No.'

'You were in a generous mood,' says she with a
little sniff. 'However, I'm glad you left Julia out
too. To bring her something, and me nothing,
would—— When you were gone, I said to myself I
had been a little mean about her, and that after all
why shouldn't she get a present if you wished to give
it? Then I thought you would hardly go to Cork
and forget me. Now—well—— Do you mean to say
you stayed hours in a town and bought nothing?'

'I have already told you so.'

'Not even anything for yourself?—a snuff-box say,

or a crutch—or,' with a saucy glance, 'a rod of iron, wherewith to reduce me to order ?'

No answer.

'It is inexplicable!' says she. 'With plenty of money in one's pocket, to so waste one's time is—— There must be something the matter with you,' with conviction; 'you are not well. Eh ?'

'Do I look ill ?' impatiently.

'You look queer, at all events,' with a careful reading of his countenance as she speaks. 'Stern. Ogreish. As if you were just going to condemn someone to the gallows.'

'My looks are unfortunate,' says he with a short laugh.

'Well—but——' She stops short, struck by an overwhelming idea. Something of the situation she has caught, and with her usual impulsiveness goes beyond it. She rises abruptly to her feet. 'I know what is in your mind,' she says ; 'you hate me. Isn't that it ?'

'Don't, Nan !' commands he with a frown. There is a terrible pain at his heart. Oh! that he could hate her ! 'I wish you would leave me,' says he, presently, conquering himself so far that his tone now is gentle, if tired to the last degree. 'You were right awhile ago. I don't feel well.'

Anything to get rid of her in his present mood! This mild falsehood takes effect.

'I knew it,' cries she, coming closer to him. 'I felt you were unlike yourself.' Her pretty face is upturned to his, and to his astonishment he sees that it has paled visibly, and that it is no common anxiety that is disturbing her.

She has a good heart, poor child, after all—he tells himself. In spite of her careless cruelty, she can feel compassion for anyone in trouble. Anyone—it does not matter whom.

'What is the matter with you?' says she. 'What has happened? Ah! you know I told you not to go to Cork without me, yet you would! You look,' wrinkling up her brows, 'like fever, I think.'

'As I told you before, my face is deceptive,' says he. 'Believe nothing that it tells you. Fever is far from me. But I have a headache; I am tired; anything you like that requires solitude. Go, Nan.' He leads her gently to the door.

'You won't let me help you then?' asks she wistfully, lingering upon the threshold.

'You could not,' says he, with mournful meaning, closing the door upon her.

She, of all others, could not help him; flinging himself into a chair he acknowledges this sad fact promptly, without troubling himself to argue about it. What madness it was in the old days to believe that love could work its way to the perfecting of a great desire! Love, that 'Mighty Lord,' as old Chaucer calls him, that little lump of leaven that sweetens all the evil upon earth, has failed Hume. There is for him no help anywhere.

He had so believed in the power of his own affection to overcome all difficulties! There is nothing anywhere so hard to repel as love, thoroughly given. We can forgive so much to the he or she who honestly likes us. Their love is a lever that lifts all barriers. They may be poor, insignificant, ungodly even—yet we condone their sins. We like them better than the *unco guid*. Some small charm we suddenly find in them, some little, little grace ridiculously out of proportion to their supposed huge

mass of faults, and because of it, we forget the rest
and take them to our hearts. And all because this
or that creature considers us the best on earth! So
vain is man!

But Nan had not been so beguiled. She had
refused to hearken to the voice of the charmer; she
had been as a deaf adder. His love had in nowise
touched her. Yet it was stronger than most. And
love surely is greater than hate, more enduring than
jealousy; yet his had failed him!

'Still here?' says Nan, thrusting her charming
head inside the door. 'How foolish! Why don't
you go upstairs and lie down? See, I've brought
you some Cologne water. Nothing so refreshing
when one's head is aching. There now,' laying her
soft saturated palm against his forehead, 'isn't that
nice?'

'Very,' says Hume miserably, pressing the kindly
little hand more closely against his brow, and then
with a sudden impulsive passion against his lips.

CHAPTER XIV.

'What should we discover, under
That seductive mask, I wonder?'

'WELL, I'll be glad when this dinner is over,' says Nan, with a little yawn. 'To-night we shall entertain our neighbours for the last time for some months, I hope ; and to-morrow—sing ho ! for London. You'll be glad to come, Pen ?'

'Rather,' says Penelope laconically. She is a very different Penelope to-day to what she was last week. Her blue eyes are brilliant, her lips red ; a very pretty colour is dying her soft cheeks.

'What ! in spite of the fact that you must leave him ?'

'Oh ! as to that,' says Penelope, the pretty colour deepening, 'he says—that perhaps—that in fact it is very likely he may be able to spare a week or two in June, and run over to see us.'

Nan laughs.

'I think it very likely, too,' says she. 'Pouf! how warm it grows! You had a hot walk up here, darling; take off your hat and rest yourself. Are they sending up your luggage?'

'Yes. It is all packed, except my dress for this evening. Oh, Nan! what a lovely dress it is! and how good you always are to me!'

'Well, as it is Freddy's last chance of seeing you until next month, I thought I'd give him something to remember,' says Nan. 'You do look nice in pink! I'll say that for you. And now, go straight upstairs, and lie down; on second thoughts I have decided that a lounge here will be of no earthly value to you, and the long journey to-morrow may knock you up, unless you are well prepared for it.'

'Is a dance the night before a preparation?'

'You mustn't dance. If the others will—and I've asked a good many for the evening—that is nothing to you. Now, Pen, do be sensible. You know you are as yet far from strong. Well, if you won't promise,

I'll certainly speak to Freddy about it. He will keep you in order.'

Penelope laughs as she gathers up her hat and prepares to leave the room.

'He has asked me to give him all the waltzes,' she says maliciously, looking back at her sister before finally closing the door; after which she runs up the broad, beautiful staircase to her room, singing to herself in a sweet voice and low, for pure lightness of a happy heart.

Nan, who would probably have followed her to remonstrate still further with her, is checked by a shadow that darkens one of the windows. Turning, she sees it is Hume, and throwing up the window, she lets him step into the library from the veranda outside.

'Where have you been?' asks she indifferently.

'At the Point. I wanted to see Leslie about that young mare. I met Julia there.'

'Yes?'—something in his tone makes her look up at him.

'She told me—— Have you heard the news about your cousin?'

'I have heard nothing. He is not ill?' anxiously.

'Not that I heard. He is going abroad, however; he has exchanged into a regiment ordered to India.'

'No!' says Nan in a long-drawn-out breath. A sense of instant relief comes to her. Thank goodness! If this be true she will be troubled with him no longer.

'Yes; it is true. Julia told me herself. He came down last night, to bid her farewell, she says.' He pauses. 'He is not leaving until to-morrow evening,' he says presently, flicking a little dust off the sleeve of his coat.

'Good gracious! And Julia is dining here to-night.'

'Yes, I suppose so.'

'But what will she do with him?'

'Bring him, I should think.'

Nan looks at him angrily.

'You are a mass of contradictions!' cries she in high wrath. 'First you spend your time accusing me of flirting with that miserable Boyle, and commanding me to desist from it, and now, when I don't want to see him at all, you turn round and order me to invite him to dinner.'

'I don't see how I was either commanding or ordering you,' says Hume. 'I merely suggested to you that, as your aunt was dining here, she would in all probability bring your cousin with her. As for my being a mass of contradictions, surely that accusation applies more to you than to me. Against my will you have encouraged Ffrench up to this, and now, when I suggest the merest act of civility towards him —one, indeed, hardly to be avoided—you are openly indignant.'

'There are a pair of us, I suppose,' says she, with a vexed smile. She pulls a few flowers out of a vase near her, and then pushes them back again impatiently. 'Well, at all events,' says she with stern determination, 'I shan't ask him to dinner.'

'No ?'

'Do you mean to say you want me to ask him ?' demands she irritably.

'Certainly not. He is the last man on earth I should care to see in my house. I have the very profoundest contempt for him,' says Hume calmly. ' But I don't see how you are to get out of it.'

' Nothing simpler, so far as I can judge. I don't ask him. He doesn't come. *V'là tout.*'

' Well, but why don't you wish to ask him ?' says Hume suddenly, turning his eyes more directly on hers.

' Places all made up,' returns she evasively.

' That isn't it, Nan.'

' No, it isn't. I've taken a dislike to him, if you must know,' with a little frown. ' Not,' with an in-born sense of honesty, 'that he has ever done any-thing to offend me. It is only that—— Really,' with a short laugh, ' I can't explain it. Put it down, if you like, to my Irish blood. Irish people are all fickle, as I dare say you have heard.'

To this Hume makes no response, but stands staring thoughtfully into the fire.

' Oh!' says Nan ; ' if you have anything on your mind, don't stand there brooding over it, but let me hear it. You think because it is his last night that he should be invited ; is that it ?'

' It does seem inhospitable,' says Hume, without

removing his gaze from the fire. 'He is, as you have often told me, not only your cousin, but a very old friend; surely he will think it strange if we send him no message ?'

'I don't see why you need imagine his thoughts for him. I might just as well manufacture them, and turn them out the other way up. Perhaps he doesn't want to come, and would look upon an invitation as a consummate bore.'

'Well, well, well,' says Hume, giving up the argument. 'So be it. No doubt you are right. We won't ask him.'

'That won't do,' says she petulantly. 'You say that only to please me—to get rid of me. You don't really think I'm right.'

'You are always right, aren't you ?'

'That won't do either. One would think I was a baby, that you talk to me so!' angrily. 'It is no use at all. If you don't think it right not to invite him, I shall have not to think it also.'

'I fail to see the necessity for that, at all events,' says Hume grimly. 'Since when has my opinion been considered infallible? One would think I was the Pope.'

'Never mind. He shall be asked!' says Mrs. Hume, with all the air of one who is determined to inflict condign punishment upon someone.

Here ensues a rather awkward pause, with which neither of them knows exactly what to do.

'It appears,' says Hume at last, 'that he has been anxious for an exchange for some time. He has been looking for it. He wants to go abroad!'

'Who told you that?'

'Mere rumour. I hardly remember, now, where I first heard it.'

'Let us hope, then, that rumour for the third or fourth time will prove true,' says she with a little sarcastic smile.

CHAPTER XV.

‘ Since we parted yester eve,
I do love thee, love, believe
Twelve times dearer, twelve hours longer,
One dream deeper, one night stronger,
One sun surer—thus much more
Than I loved thee, love, before.'

*   *   *   *   *

DINNER is well over, and dancing in the fine old hall has commenced. It is now, indeed, in full swing. Round and round move the pretty forms. Higher and sweeter sound the fiddles. Old Jack Leslie at the upper end is beating time with all his might, one hand on the other.

Ffrench, who has secured a very unwilling Nan for his partner, is waltzing as he so well knows how, and presently, the local musicians showing signs of fatigue, draws her into a room on his left, out of which leads a conservatory. Glad to terminate the dance under any pretext, she goes with him willingly enough, and, sinking on to a low lounge, beckons him to take the place beside her.

After all, she argues with herself, why should she not be civil to him for these few last remaining hours? In spite of his many faults, and the undeniable fact that he has of late become an unmitigated bore —a thing more difficult to pardon than would be a whole multitude of sins—is he not still a man and a cousin ?

She pushes her skirts aside, and invites him by glance and kindly gesture, to take half her seat. The kindliness is fatal; the friendly glance is misunderstood. Ffrench—distracted by the thought of his near departure, his nerves strung to the highest pitch; the resolution to speak to her, to induce her to accompany him to his foreign home, that has been with him all day, now too strong to be controlled— refuses the offered seat, but stands before her, gazing down at her in all his fatuity, his dark eyes glowing with but ill-repressed excitement.

It seems to him that now, at last, his hour has

come. Her unloved home, her detested husband, all the wretchedness of her daily life—so well understood by him, as he believes—must speak for him. Surely she will be glad to exchange it all for a life of love with him. And after awhile, when a divorce has been obtained, and she is indeed his wife, the past will be forgotten, the hideous first union, as loveless as it was undesired, would be thrust out of sight, and he and she would know happiness together. All those early sordid considerations that had marked his former affection for her, and had so much to do with Julia's approval or disapproval of his marriage with Nan, have been finally flung overboard, and only a wild, reckless passion lives. Strong in his belief that she is more than indifferent to Hume, and therefore willing to escape from him at any price, he builds securely on his hope of gaining a consent to the plan that will for ever place a stigma on her character. And yet, selfish as he is, there is so much real affection for her in his breast that to condemn him wholly is impossible. His folly amounts to madness as he stands there, gazing down on her pretty, pure, clever face, and deliberately tells himself she is capable of such an act as he would incite her to perform.

'Sit down,' says Nan, with an affectation of light-ness, though her heart has begun to beat with a rather uncomfortable haste as she notes his silence, and the glow in his eyes fixed immovably on hers. What on earth is he going to do now? Was there ever so impossible a person? 'Don't stand there glowering down upon me. One would think you were a ghoul,' says she, changing colour in spite of herself.

'I have something to say to you; I may as well say it at once,' says he slowly but feverishly.

'Oh, don't,' says Nan, rising precipitately; 'there's lots of time. Put it off till to-morrow. I'll be at home at three, at twelve, at one, at any hour. Yes, one. Come to lunch—do.'

There is something almost pathetic in this hospit-able invitation.

'You ean hear me as well now as then,' says Ffrench, who has grown 'abominably white,' as Nan afterwards described it to—well, to someone. 'No,' violently. 'Don't go; don't stir. I *will* speak.'

Unconsciously, perhaps, but yet with force, he lays his hands upon her arms, and presses her back into her seat. She would have gone, but this act detains her. A quick, haughty anger wakes within her. *Let him speak, then.* She would have spared him, but—— How *dares* he touch her so!

'Well, speak!' says she, in a little low grating voice.

And he does speak, with a vengeance, and without an interruption. Nan, with her face bent slightly downwards, and her fan lying listless on her knees, hears throughout the wild unbridled tale he tells her, and not until he has come to an end makes so much as an ejaculation. She is as white as he is when it is over, and at last she lifts her head. Some girls would have been frightened by such an outburst, some shamed, some grieved. Nan is indignant, *pur et simple.*

'Well,' says she, looking up at him with suspiciously brilliant eyes. Something in their expression puzzles him, there is generally a little sense of uncertainty before one fully awakes.

'I could speak for ever, but now you know all. You know that——'

'And how about your love for Penelope ?'

'Did you take me seriously, then,' says he, dense still, and now imagining her jealous ; 'I said that merely for a purpose : to hide, to conceal for the time being, all I felt for you. Surely for one moment you did not think my love for you had cooled. Oh, Nan, you must have known better than that. You must have known that my very soul was yours.' Here he takes her hand, pressing it passionately between both his own, but she wrenches it free.

'Are you mad ?' says she. 'Or is it—is it,' half choking, 'because you think the shadow of that old scandal about my hasty marriage still hangs over me, that you talk to me like this ?' She is conscious of a feeling of faintness as she says this ; her hands have grown cold, her throat dry. Her marriage ! It is impossible not to think of it just now, and equally impossible to put into words all the thoughts about it that throng her mind. Oh, that there had been no whispering about it—that it had been as the marriage of other girls ! That—that no one could be at liberty to judge of it, as hateful to her—as an act of gross injustice.

'It is quite impossible that you should accuse me of direct insult towards you,' says Ffrench sullenly. 'You have known me too long for that. I speak as I think merely—as I believe. I am no dealer in sweet phrases or pretty words. I have not learned to gloss over the rough bits of life. And what is to be gained by such hypocrisy? I love you. I say that plainly, though it may offend at the first blush. Why should it? It is the truth. And you—well—at all events, you do not love your husband.'

He pauses and looks at her defiantly. Some terrible contention within her renders her dumb. One feeling alone is defined, that she hates Boyle with all her heart for having forced this question upon her. How dare he ask her if she does or does not love her husband!

'You are silent,' says he triumphantly. 'Nan, Nan, are you going to let your whole life go, without knowing what love means? This man Hume, what is he to you?—a mere name, and worse. He has destroyed your happiness. Deliberately he planned that yachting excursion to——'

'I will not hear you speak so of my husband,' says

Nan coldly. ' I will not listen to you whilst you are in this mood. It is a very fortunate thing that you have made up your mind to go to India, as—a very little more of this kind of thing, and I should forbid you my house.'

' Why should you act the hypocrite to me ?' says he. ' To others—to the outside world, if you will— but to me ! And to speak of him so, as my husband, maddens *me.* You know in your heart that you detest him, as, as I do. Curse him ! Was not the whole wide world before him, with money enough to go where he would and marry whom he chose, that he should come down to this little quiet village and steal you away from one who could have made you happy.'

' Meaning you ?' asks she calmly.

' Yes,' defiantly. ' I could ; and I alone, I firmly believe. Deny it if you will now, but—you *did* care for me.' He pauses, and then, falsely encouraged by her strange silence, he says in a low tone—' You *do.*'

Nan laughs. Not a pleasant laugh, but one full of bitterness and contempt.

' My manners must be exquisite indeed, to quite an

unusual degree, if you ever imagined that,' says she slowly. 'I liked you. Yes. I tolerated your many faults because you were my cousin and an old friend. Quite true; but as to caring for you in the sense you mean'—she stops short and turns suddenly a pale indignant face full on his—'if you were the last man on earth,' says she quickly enough now, 'I would not marry you; I *never* would have married you!'

'Wait a moment,' says he hoarsely. 'Do not say another word. You do not understand yet all that is in my mind. You cannot blind me to the fact that your life here is wretched, unbearable almost. Then why not cast it behind you. Look here, Nan, I start for India next week; why not come with me? Cut adrift this log to which you are chained, and in time —when a divorce can be claimed—we——'

As smart a box on his ear as ever he got in his life puts a termination to this sentence. Involuntarily Ffrench lifts his hand to his cheek, while Nan, whose breath is coming in little hurried gasps through her lips, confronts him, pale with passion, of the honest, orthodox sort.

'There!' says she, with a beautiful simplicity that might well have marked her martial exploits of ten years ago. Nothing more is possible for her to say, because she is trembling with agitation, and a little shame perhaps, because grown-up married people should not 'delight to bark and bite' as children and dogs are popularly supposed to do. And, besides, her eyes are full of tears, and her pretty hands clasped together us though demanding support one from the other.

It is now Ffrench's turn to laugh, and he does it quite as successfully as she did, five minutes ago. There is, however, a little savagery in his forced amusement.

'That is so like you!' he says, which is a rather unfortunate compliment. 'Yet, even so, you do not deceive me. I should have given you more time to think it over. It has come as a shock to you now, but——'

'Boyle!' says she suddenly. So suddenly, indeed, and with such a stamp of her foot, that perforce he sinks into silence. Having so far conquered him, she advances upon him about an inch or so and then

stands still again. 'Don't be a fool!' says she with
more eloquence than elegance, it must be confessed
—but one can forgive her. 'I tell you that not now,
or in the past, or in any possible future, could I
regard you as being other than one whom it would
be out of my power to more than tolerate. I am not
shocked, as you suppose; I am only disgusted : see
here,' with a little contemptuous movement of her
hand—'you ask me to give up my life here, to—to
forsake my husband—to follow your fortunes through
the world—for what? What do you offer me in exchange for all I should give up? What should I
gain?' There is a scorn that is almost cruel in the
closed mouth and the clear eyes as she asks these
unromantic questions.

'Nothing, it seems,' says he with a sharp indrawing
of his breath. At last the real truth—or part of it—
has begun to dawn upon him. He was wrong all
through, then! She had deceived him from start to
finish. She had never really cared for him ; but as
surely she had not cared for Hume. There is a sort
of fierce comfort in this thought, even at this hour.
'You gain little by remaining, either. This man

whom you call "husband," do you imagine that the
mere paltry bodily comforts by which he ties you to
him will suffice you to the end ? I have been,' with
a sudden shrinking as if from fleshly pain, ' mistaken
in you, but not so far as that. You are not so
material as you would describe yourself. In the
end—at last—when you tire of loveless luxury, you
may regret to-night.'   ⸱

'That is true,' says she. 'I shall always regret
it. It has killed my regard for one who was almost a
brother to me.' A look of great distress has grown
upon her face. She turns her head anxiously
towards the door, as if expecting—rather unreason-
ably—some succour from it.

'He won't come,' says Ffrench slowly, with a
hateful smile, who has read her secret hope, and has
been utterly demoralized by it. 'I am afraid he is
not thinking so much about you as you fondly
believe.' Then all at once his sneering tone vanishes,
and reality in the shape of violence takes its place.
See here,' says he : 'I called you a hypocrite a
while since, not believing. Now you wake my
doubts. Come, tell me this. You cast me off with a

word or two, as though I am beneath your notice. What of him, eh ? Of Hume ? Are you prepared to say you love him ? Now then, Nan,' with a hoarse laugh, 'the truth—the truth, you know, and nothing but the truth.'

' Hear it then,' says she flashing round at him. ' I do love him.'

She has faced him as she says it, her eyes uplifted to his ; but the words once past her lips, and sounding on the air, she feels inwardly as though she were shrinking back within herself. The blood mounts heavily to her brow, and lingers there. Her heart is beating so loudly that she can hear it. Is it a lie, or can there be truth in that strange sentence she has uttered ?

Truth ! Courage grows within her.

' Who are you, that you should judge him ?' cries she, in a choking tone. ' Is he not as worthy of love as another ? Why, then, should it be denied him ? Supposing,' with a last terrible touch of remorseful uncertainty, 'that I didn't love him, should I not be the most ungrateful wretch alive ? I——'

' That will do,' says Ffrench, with a touch of com-

mand. ' You have convinced me. There is no want
of further argument. The victory is his—mine the
defeat. I acknowledge it : even you in his interest
cannot demand more. If you have learned to love
your captor,' with a bitter smile, ' I should be the last
to——'

' There, not another word,' says Nan, interrupting
him with a little imperious gesture. She sweeps
past him towards the door that will lead her once
more to where they are dancing, talking, making
merry for all the world to see, and where privacy is
unknown. She is glad to get back to them. Her
throat seems on fire, her eyes desirous of those tears
she must deny them. Yet, strange contradiction, a
secret longing for the people to depart, and leave her
free to think out this startling new problem that has
presented itself, renders her feverish. Thus she
would shun self-examination, and yet court it.

A little seat just inside the hall—where the dancing
is still going on—being empty, she drops into it,
feeling tired both mentally and physically. Her face
is very white, and the little doubt as to whether anything is worth one's while to bother about, that comes

to us all at times, renders the corners of her lips forlorn.

Hume, who has been dancing with one of the Leslie girls, looking casually in her direction, notes all this, and promptly transferring his partner to a more eligible, and therefore more desirable, *parti*, crosses the room to where the poor, pretty hostess sits, morally crushed and crumpled.

CHAPTER XVI.

'And grief shall come with womanhood.'

*　　　*　　　*　　　*　　　*

'YOU look idle,' says Hume, smiling down at her,
yet there is trouble in the smile. 'May I have the
pleasure of this dance?'

'Oh! do you want to dance it?' asks she in a tone
so nervous, so reluctant, so pleading, so altogether
unlike the usual Nan who would once have refused
him without a qualm, that his suspicion of her being
in distress grows into a certainty.

'Yes, I do,' says he; and to his surprise she rises
and yields herself to him, and presently they lose
themselves among the other dancers.

Once before she had danced with him, but never
since her marriage. And now, as she feels his arms
round her, a sense of security, rest, peace, falls on

her. Surely he is strong to defend her from all harm, all insults. She has but to call on him, and he will answer.

All at once the goodness of him comes home to her. Was there ever one single hour when he had not been her friend ; he had borne with her coldness, injustice, temper, without complaining. He had given himself up to her : to gain what ?—ingratitude !

She had said awhile since that she loved him ! Her heart beats fast as she remembers that. Was it a lie ? Or was it—— Oh no, impossible ! after all she had said, done ; and, besides, it is too late——

Hume, becoming conscious that she is trembling in his embrace, looks hastily down at her, and to his horror and alarm finds she is crying, silently but passionately. She has turned her face slightly inwards against his sleeve, as though to hide it.

Managing so as to bring their dance to a termination at an open doorway, where fortunately no one is standing, he takes her hurriedly into the diningroom, and closes the door behind him.

' Now, not a word—not a word,' says he quickly, seeing her about to speak. ' Sit there and drink this.' Pouring her out a glass of sherry, and handing it to her.

'Oh,' says she in great distress, 'I don't know what has happened to me! How can I go back to them now? They will see I have been crying.'

'Not if you don't cry any more. Try and control yourself; or—why go back? I can make excuses for you.'

'No—no!' hastily; 'I must return. I would not have—— There is a reason——' She pauses as if uncertain.

'If there is,' regarding her keenly, 'you must, of course, come back.'

'If,' nervously, 'I might explain——'

'Not now,' decisively. 'Afterwards, if you wish it. But,' with an unavoidable touch of hauteur, 'not then, either, unless it is your own desire. Now, do drink that. There! you are better now, are you not? That's right.'

'I hardly know what is the matter with me,' says she in a little shamed way; and then impulsively, 'Oh yes, I do know: I have been disturbed, distressed by——'

'No—now. Not a word, indeed. Do you forget your guests have still a claim upon you? They must go soon, however, and then you can do as you like.' Something in his manner tells her he is determined not to accept from her any impulsive communication. 'Old Lady Cashelmore spoke of going ten minutes ago. Come, I dare say she is looking for you now, to make her adieu.'

'But can I go like this?' says she, springing up and examining herself in a mirror. 'Oh no! they will notice me; they will think all sorts of things.'

'Nonsense! They will notice nothing. You are almost yourself again. A summer shower like that leaves few traces.' He is trying to speak cheerfully, though secretly unhinged by a desire to learn the cause of her distress.

'But my eyes,' says she, turning her face up to his, that he may give an opinion as to their fitness for the prying gaze of society, 'they are red, aren't they?'

'Not at all. You would scarcely know that even one tear had dimmed them.'

'Are you sure?' in a rather forsaken little voice,
and still with those melancholy and most lovely
features pleading to him for a kind sentence. Oh
that he dared take her in his arms, and kiss from
them their last faint dews !

'They are all right, I assure you,' says he, in a
terribly prosaic way, born of his forbidden longing to
be demonstrative. 'Come,`let us get rid of these
people as quickly as possible ; you need not talk
much. For this one night I will try to do your
manners and my own.'

He is smiling, but she is looking at him seriously,
thoughtfully, and as she thinks, the tears rise once
again to her eyes.

'Thank you,' she says gently.

Half an hour later, even the most determined leech
in the way of guests has taken his departure—I'm
bound to confess that that terrible reptile belongs, as
a rule, to the gender feminine. Hume having done
his duty nobly to the last, gives a distinct sigh of
satisfaction as the man closes the hall-door, and,
turning, finds Nan beside him.

'Well, they are gone at last !' says she wearily.

'An incontrovertible fact,' returns he, speaking lightly, but with his eyes fixed on hers. 'You are tired—you have a journey before you to-morrow. Take my advice, and go straight to bed.'

'You won't let me tell you about it, then,' says she, when she has silently returned his gaze for a second or two.

'If you wish to tell me, I should like to hear,' says Hume gravely. He leads the way to the library, and she follows him.

CHAPTER XVII.

'She is so pretty, so sweet and dear,
There's many a lover who loves her well :
I may not hope, I can only fear,
Yet shall I venture my love to tell ?
Ah ! I have pleaded, and not in vain,
Though she's so pretty and I am so plain.'

A BRIGHT fire is burning in the grate ; Hume, taking up the poker, stirs it to a brisker blaze. It hardly requires it, but a little time in certain cases is greatly to be desired. Nan's unwonted gentleness towards him, her depression, a new, untranslatable expression on her mobile face, all have disturbed him, and lead him to fear—what, he hardly knows.

'Sit down,' he says abruptly, pushing a chair towards her.

'No ; it is hardly worth while. I shan't keep you long. I——' She comes to a full stop.

Hume, quitting his position on the hearthrug, goes up to her.

'If you don't want to confide in me, Nan, why compel yourself to do it ?' his tone is perhaps a little brusque.

'But I do want to tell you. Only it is so hard,' says she, raising her eyes for an instant, and then lowering them again. 'It—it is about Boyle. He——' (long pause). 'Oh !' throwing out her hands in an agony of impatience and shame, ' I don't know how to tell you.'

'You needn't. I understand him perfectly,' says Hume icily. 'Pray do not distress yourself. There, go to bed. As I told you before, you want rest. Go and sleep off this fit of depression that has taken possession of you.'

'If I want to get either rest or sleep, I must get this thing off my mind,' says she dejectedly. 'I must speak to somebody, and,' with deepening melancholy, 'there is only you.'

' A misfortune indeed !' with a growing feeling of bitterness. 'Don't you think you could live until to-morrow gives you an opportunity of speaking to Penelope ?'

'Does that mean that you won't listen to me?'
To his astonishment, her eyes have filled with tears.
There is keen reproach in her glance. He had expected her to walk out of the room in a small fury
at his rudeness, or whatever she might choose to
call it, and here she stands before him, with only a
mournful surprise on her charming face. It undoes
him.

'Of course I will listen,' says he, throwing himself
into a chair, with all the air of one who is prepared
for anything. In truth, his heart has sunk a little.
It must be some terrible confession that could bring
so much weakness to her. Will she never speak?
Now that he has declared his desire to hear all she
may have to say, power to tell anything seems to
have deserted her. She is standing over there,
motionless and as white as nervous emotion can
make anybody.

'Well, is it too much for you?' asks he, at last
(in a horrid sarcastic sort of way), as she doesn't
scruple to tell him afterwards.

'Do you know,' begins she, recovering her spirits
somewhat, and directing one of the old wrathful

glances at him, which extraordinary fact is now intensely welcome to him. She is still the old Nan— his Nan—in spite of the world. No influence has been strong enough to alter that quick, impertinent, short-lived temper. And there is besides a wild relief in the thought that the penitent mood had not gone deep, by which one might argue that the cause for penitence must necessarily be small. 'Do you know,' says she, 'I've always said it, mind you, and I think so still, that you are one of the most hateful people I ever met; at all events, you are a very hard person to tell things to?'

'Am I?' says he, springing to his feet. 'I believe I am. But I won't be so any longer. Now, go on ; tell me everything. I declare to you that, in spite of my manner, I am dying to hear all you have to tell.'

Thus encouraged, she makes open confession, which, let us hope, is good for her soul, and confides to him all that Ffrench had said to her, and a good deal of what she said to him : all he had done to her— that compelling her to reseat herself and listen to him had rankled in her mind—and all she had done to him, with one trifling exception.

'Oh, you were right,' she winds up, deep contrition in her voice and the bend of her pretty head. 'You always said he was in love with me still, and I suppose he was, if,' contemptuously, 'one can call that sort of thing love.'

'It is the name a great many people will give it,' says Hume. 'Why shouldn't you? After all, the orthodox, humdrum sort of devotion doesn't suit you. And Ffrench is a good-looking man.'

This last little foolish speech is an unconscious betrayal of how he has envied that other man the beauty of which Nature to him has been so niggardly.

'Is he?' says Nan, as if awakening to a new fact. 'Oh, well,' indifferently, 'I dare say it didn't occur to me,' after which she relapses once more into melancholy.

'Where is he?' asks Hume abruptly.

'Gone, thank goodness,' says she. 'Pen told me. He saw her almost directly after, you know,' with a little flush, 'and he bade her good-bye, and said he was starting by the early train for Cork. He must have driven all the way to Bandon. And you know he embarks almost immediately. I really think,' says she in, a relieved tone, 'that he is gone for good and all.'

Hume turns abruptly aside. A wild longing to catch the fellow and give him a horse-whipping not to be forgotten had taken his fancy for a grim moment—a moment in which the thought of having him in his power and being able to half kill him was sweet. And then the revulsion came with the certainty that he could not only half kill, but kill him outright if he so chose. That slight, weak fool! And to drag her name in! No; it was not to be thought of. But somehow his anger towards her rose higher within him as he felt how she debarred him from a pleasure that would have been brutal, but intense.

'Well,' he says, turning to her savagely, although his heart is beating at the sight of her standing so pale, so penitent, beneath the light of the lamps, 'what is to be the end of all this? He is gone; but the world is full of vermin such as he. How are you going to defend yourself in the future? I am nothing to you; you have therefore no protector—at least, not one to whom you would care to come—to save yourself from these annoyances.'

'I have come to you now,' says she in a little low voice.

'Yes; but only, as you took care to tell me'—with a quick frown—'because there was no one else near. That sort of thing won't last.'

' But——' begins she confusedly.

There is no knowing now what she meant to say, because she is fiercely interrupted by him. The quiet man whom she had believed she was tied to has disappeared; a vehement man unguarded in his language has taken his place.

'You will never care for me,' he says. 'I have made up my mind to that. It'—turning a white, troubled face to hers—'it would have been a thousand times better for you that you had never seen me, and married Ffrench.'

' You said something like that before,' says she, flashing at him a glance full of terrible meaning. 'If you really think it, say now, say clearly, that you regret you ever married me!'

There is so great a touch of despair in her eyes,

that, though hardly understanding the significance of it, it steadies him.

'No!' says he sharply, grief and strong passion blended in his tone. 'Beyond all that God has given me, I thank Him for you. My regret is for you alone. With me you are not happy ; with him——'

'What folly!' cries she, interrupting him with impatience. 'I tell you, if he had been the owner of that yacht, and I had been compelled to choose be-tween him and the cruel gossip of my county, I should have chosen the gossip. As it was,' lowering her voice, 'I chose you.'

Surely, in all conscience, this is encouragement enough, but he has been too long denied all privileges to be able at once to grasp the flag of truce, however earnestly held out.

'I never did you the injustice to believe you could love him,' says he coldly. 'He has, however, so much power over you—he can make you cry.'

'No,' with quick denial. 'No, he cannot.'

She hesitates, and, as if ashamed of her last words, blushes a hot crimson. Then the nervous tide flows away, leaving her very white.

'Do you think I have forgotten?' asks Hume impatiently. 'Why, it was in my very arms that——'

'Nevertheless, you are wrong. It was not he who made me cry,' interrupts she in a tone that is scarcely audible.

'Not he? who, then?'

'You!' cries she suddenly, in a little sharp, broken voice that has yet some fierceness in it.

'I?'

Her agitation has communicated itself to him. He has drawn nearer to her, his face scarcely less white than her own.

'Yes, you—you! What I mean is——'

She breaks off as if not knowing how to go on, and begins to drum nervously with the tips of her fingers upon the table near her. Her eyes are following the fantastic movements of her fingers; her whole face is full of a supreme trouble. Hume, who is hardly breathing, and who dares not believe, watches her in terrible uncertainty.

Suddenly she bursts into tears, and covers her face with her hands.

'Think what you will,' cries she, with angry passion. 'But when I felt your arms round me that time—that time you speak of—I thought—I felt—I knew that I loved you!'

His arms are round her again now, and somehow hers have this time found their way round him, and if he doesn't cry too, he is certainly so very near it that it is beyond doubt that there are tears in his eyes—and altogether they are both as happy as anyone in the world could wish them.

*   *   *   *   *

After a little while, when they have descended from their seventh heaven to their sixth, Nan, whose smiles are never very far from her tears, glances up at him roguishly from beneath her long lashes, with a pretty soft laugh that is irresistible.

'Well, what is it?' asks he, when he has kissed the mischievous lips, and subsided with their owner into a huge armchair, big enough to hold a small family.

'Oh, nothing!' says she, growing rather shamefaced as at some hardly creditable recollection. 'At

least, not much. Only something that recurred to me
—something I had done. A horrid thing !'   .

'I don't believe it,' says Hume promptly.

'But I did it really. I—oh I'd hate to tell you ;
but perhaps,' naïvely, 'I'd better—eh ?'

'Much better. If you tell me everything, I'll tell
you everything. Come, now ; that's a bargain.'

'But you—what have you to tell ?' asks she quickly,
looking round at him, and proceeding to study his
features with a jealous determination to pierce his
heart and drag his secrets to the light that enchants
him.

'A mere trifle—a small thing. The most ordinary
confession,' declares he, with much criminating pro-
testation of glance and gesture.

'Oh, George !' says she, and nothing more ; but
three volumes could not have contained the reproaches
found therein.

'Never mind. Go on, and "make your sowl first,"
—that's what they say here, isn't it ?—and I'll make
mine afterwards.'

Reassured by the gaiety of his tone—it is only the
most hardened criminals who can jest with the rope

round their necks—Nan plucks up courage and proceeds to unburden her mind.

' It is about Boyle again,' says she.

' Oh, bother him !' says Hume with deep disgust.

' Well — that's it.   I did bother him.   I don't
believe he knew where he was for a moment or two
after I—boxed his ears !'

' What !   Did you do that ?   Boxed his ears ?'
exclaims Hume, starting to his feet, and leaving her
alone in the small family mansion.

' Yes ; it was dreadful, wasn't it ?' says Nan,
abashed.   ' But I couldn't help it, indeed.   It was
done before I had time to think whether it would be
a nice sort of thing to do or not.   I'm afraid I hurt
him too !   Oh, I wish I hadn't done it !   It was so
unladylike, wasn't it, now ?   So, so rough.   Just like
one of the boys.   As I said, it was horrid !'

' It was the thing of all others to do,' cries he,
laughing heartily.   ' A noble deed.   And so you
vanquished him.   Alone you did it ?   There is only
one thing to be regretted,' taking her pretty hand
and pressing it to his lips.   ' That this should have
been contaminated by touching him.'

' Well, that's over,' says Nan. ' My confession is made, and now,' regarding him somewhat uneasily, ' for yours. I know I have not behaved well to you, but I thought, I believed, that you—— Well, hurry, get it over. I dare say,' with a sigh, ' I'll forgive you.'

' I dare say,' retorts he sardonically. He catches her hands and draws her up out of the chair into his arms and gives her a mighty hug. ' There is only this,' says he, ' that you are my first love, and will be my last love, and that I don't believe there is a woman on earth worth looking at except yourself.'

CHAPTER XVIII.

' Oh ! to see her with the baby !'

A YEAR has gone by. A whole, long sweet, happy year for Nan ; and once again a new spring has been born.

Something else, too, has been born—a little son to Nan. A jolly, lusty little chap, now six weeks old ; so dear a thing, so priceless a treasure, that both the father and mother of it regard it with a respectful rapture that borders upon awe. It might even have suggested itself to the interested observer, gazing with a cynical eye upon their slavish worship of the atom lying in the elaborate bassinette, that they had for· gotten the fact that one or two other people had had a baby before them.

Had the observer told them this, they would pro-

bably have cried in chorus : ' Oh yes ; but not such
a baby ! Not such a prince among his fellows !' And
where would the observer have been then ? Would he
have had the courage or the knowledge to contradict
them ? And even if a desire for truth at any cost had
driven him to be so ill-bred as to do so, what would
he have gained by it ? Briefly and sarcastically—
nothing.

As for Hume, up to this the world had contained
for him his wife only ; now his vision enlarged a little,
and he saw his child. It was a revelation, and a dear
one. He had waited long, but his life was the fuller
for waiting. By night he dreamed of it, and by day
he thanked God for this last, this unsurpassable gift
of His—the little child.

After the birth of this small hero, his wife had
been far from strong. She had pined a good deal
indeed, and declined to take hold of the vigorous life
that once had been hers, and had in fact succeeded in
frightening the life out of her husband by her seeming
inability to lift herself out of the languor that had
seized upon her. But all that now is a thing of the
past ; colour once again has crept into her cheeks, fire

to the lovely eyes. For the past week she has been given permission to see any friends to whom she may wish to show the 'most beautiful child in the world,' and to-day she is to go for her first drive,—to Rathmore, needless to say—where Penelope, who has been for six months Mrs. Croker, is staying with her husband.

Just now Mrs. Hume and nurse are bending over the 'young master,' seeing to the tying of the elaborate sash that covers pretty nearly all his small body, and stands out like two azure wings at his back.

'An' an angel he is too, God bless him !' says nurse, bestowing a resounding smack upon the tiny cheek.

'Here's Mr. Hume,' says Nan, whose quick ear, love-trained by this time, has heard the approaching footsteps of her husband. 'Who is with him, I wonder ? There, that will do, nurse; you can go now and dress yourself, and be ready the moment I call you.'

'Shall I take baby, ma'am ?'

'No ; leave him to me. The master will want to see him,' with a little smile, and a cuddle for baby, who distinctly resents it.

'I've brought you an old friend, Nan,' says Hume, putting his head into his wife's boudoir; 'one who has called many a time and oft, and who is most anxious to see you.'

'What? Murphy?' says Nan, with a little cry of delight. 'Is it really you, Murphy? Oh, come in; you know they wouldn't let me see you before; but I've been dying to show you baby all the time.'

She holds out her hands to him, and Murphy, all aglow with pride and delight, and with his withered old face a sight to see because of the creases and wrinkles accentuated a thousand-fold by reason of his irrepressible smiles, advances towards her.

'You never saw such a nice baby,' says Nan, as if she couldn't help it, and then, overcome by all the love and joy that has filled her life, she stoops forward and, slipping her arm round the faithful old friend's neck, presses her cheek to his.

'Well,' says Hume. 'After that I suppose I may consider myself *de trop?*'

'Yes, yes; go away, and let me have a chat with Murphy,' says his wife, for the first time since her heart spoke for him, resigned to his absence. Truly, had Murphy only known it, he was a favoured friend. Hume with a slight grimace quits the room, leaving Nan at leisure to exhibit the marvellous infant who deigns to call her mother, to the admiring Murphy.

And Murphy is quite equal to the occasion ; he seems positively born to it. His raptures over the proudly indifferent infant are as loud and almost as sincere as Nan's own, which is saying a great deal. He is not entirely satisfied, indeed, until the young gentleman in question is given into his sole custody, and sitting in a low chair the old man dandles and nurses him with a world of content in his small un-faded eyes.

'It's for all the world as if I'd gone back twinty years, an' had yerself on me knee,' says he. 'Ah, ye'h ! look at him now, how he howlds on to me finger ! 'Tis as sthrong as a horse, he is. I do love babies, miss. 'Pon my fegs I do. There's somethin' so nate an' so cunnin' about thim. They're the divil's own smart cratures ! Oh ! musha ; but I wish the poor misthress was alive now to see this darlint ; 'tis she'd be the proud lady intirely. But 'twasn't to be.' He sighs softly. A touch of grief ages his face

—for a minute only—then, the baby giving a vigorous kick, recalls him to the happy present. 'Look at him,' says he, chuckling gloriously, and with a sort of proprietary pride in the thriving atom on his knee. 'Was there iver the like of him? Look at him now, wid the eyes boultin' out of his head, and all wid the cleverness of him. Ye were all smart, faith, an' as for him!—Och,' with a prolonged roar of laughter, 'Oh—ha—ha—ha; faix, 'tis winkin' at me he is. Wisha more power to ye, asthore,' to the child; 'sure, what's the ould man for but to be made fun of by the likes of you? Well, Miss Nan, I must say but this child's a credit to ye.'

'I'm so glad you like him,' says Nan. 'He is a beauty, isn't he?'

'He is that, miss, sure. But 'tisn't only that,' says Murphy seriously. 'There's other things. Beauty's a fine thing, but juty is finer still, an' it can't be said but ye've done yours. Wid a big estate awaitin' an heir, 'twas the right thing for you to go an' have a son—an' ye done it. Great praise is due to ye. I'was the dacentest, the most respectable thing I ever heard o' ye. There was twinty chances to one 'twould have

bin a girl, but ye overcame iverything, miss, an' had
yer boy.'

'Oh, Murphy!' cries Miss Nan, who is now laughing uncontrollably ; 'it is you, and not my son, who
are the "divil's own smart crature." There, sit down
now, and nurse him awhile. It gives me a rest, do
you see.' She rings the bell energetically. 'Now
you shall have a tumbler of punch with me,' says
she, 'if only to wish baby luck.'

'My dear, now, 'tis a dale o' throuble,' says Mr.
Murphy apologetically, to whom punch is as rare as
it is dear.

'There is no such word as trouble where your
comfort is concerned,' says she, smiling at him.
'And you know you have had a long cold walk up
here.' And presently all the necessary ingredients
for the insidious drink promised, standing on a table
at her elbow, she proceeds to make it.

'Now, you shall mind baby whilst I brew it,' says
she, 'with my own fair fingers, too, mind that ; 'twill
make it nectar, or, at least, it should. And whilst I
brew, tell me all the news. The others come and go,
and tell me what will please me, but you I can depend

upon. Papa, now, for example : let us begin with him. He is well ?'

'Tough, miss. Tough as iver. An' his eyes as bright as that " wandherin jewel " ye used to be tellin' me about. 'Tis the wondher how he goes on year afther year, an' niver a hair out of him. That'll be enough lemon, miss—ma'am, I main, but faix, 'tis hard to remimber it ; wid ye there overnigh me, lookin' for all the world like a little colleen.'

'Flatterer !' says Mrs. Hume, making a little face at him. ' There now, give me back baby, and drink long life and happiness to him.'

This ceremony having been gone through, Nan continues her examination.

'And Aunt Julia. She was here yesterday, and I thought her looking pale—put out, you know.'

'Arrah, shure she's always quare like that. Not but what she's raison for it this time. The captain has gone agin her terribly.'

'What! Boyle ?'

'Yes, miss—ma'am. Didn't they tell ye ? Faix, maybe 'tis puttin' me foot in it, I am. There, now, niver mind. I'll be tellin' it to you some other time.'

'No; go on. Nonsense, Murphy! I'm quite well now, and I won't be treated like a baby, or a lunatic any longer. What has Boyle done?'

'Fegs, me dear, from what I can gather, he's been playin' ould Harry wid his prospicts. Nothin' but the colonel's wife would do him. Boulted wid her, he did, an' carried her off to some hills, I think they said, though what they were goin' to do on the top of a cowld mountain is more than I can come at. But India is as hot as—— H'm! I beg yer pardon, me dear!' says Mr. Murphy, blushing politely and coughing behind his hand with quite unexampled good breeding. 'What I'm thinking is, that maybe 'twas one o' them burnin' mountains, an' campin' out there might be warm even in winther.'

'Ran away to the hills, with his colonel's wife! Oh, surely, Murphy—— Well, bad as he was, I never thought that of him!' Here she grows reflective, and a past bad moment or two in a conservatory returns to her. If thus to her, why not to another? But the degradation of it! Her heart burns hotly within her.

'There, now, don't put yerself out,' says Mr. Murphy

philosophically. 'Some's good, some's bad. We must have 'em of all sorts ; an' when the bad's as far away as India 'tis aisy enough to bear, though he may be a cousin.'

'Does Penelope know ?'

'Mrs. Croker? Yes, miss. They all know. I'm thinkin',' with a troubled glance, 'that 'tis kilt intirely I'll be for tellin' you about it.'

'They shan't know. I'll fool them a little bit, as they've fooled me,' says Mrs. Hume with a touch of malice. 'And now—— Oh, is that you, nurse ? Is it time to start ?'

'Yes'm. The carriage is at the door.'

'Then come, Murphy ; I'll drive you back. Nurse, take baby. Catherine, my cloak. Is that you, George ? Oh no, I won't be smothered ; I won't, indeed. One fur cloak is enough for any poor soul this heavenly day.'

CHAPTER XIX.

‘ They step, are dancing toward the bound
   Between the child and woman,
And thoughts and feelings more profound,
   And other years are coming.

‘ There is such glory in thy face,
   What can the meaning be ?
I love my love, because I know
   My love loves me !’

PENELOPE'S greeting of Nan and her son is on the
surface all it ought to be, and yet it lacks something.
There is a repressed fire in Mrs. Croker's eyes that
speaks of words kept back, with a determination that
is pain and grief to her. She pays the baby every
attention, but it's not of the undivided sort to which
his mother has been accustomed, and she resents it.
What on earth is the matter with Penelope, and
where is Gladys ? Her nephew is on the spot, and

yet she has not rushed to embrace him. Have they all gone mad?

'You are tired,' says Penelope in a tone that admits of no contradiction, the moment nurse has retired with baby.

'I'm not,' says Nan.

'Yes, you are. Come in here,' opening a door. 'We shall be alone here.'

Good heavens! What has happened? Her vague suspicions of something having gone wrong, were then correct. Has Freddy— But no! Any other man but not Freddy!

'What do you think has happened?' says Mrs. Croker, pressing her sister into a cosy chair, and looking down at her. 'Only this morning, too. You'll never guess.'

'I don't want to speak,' gasps Nan, expecting the end of all things.

'Lord Cashelmore came over after breakfast and proposed to Gladys—to that baby—and she has accepted him.'

Nan leans back and roars with laughter, partly with relief, partly with amusement.

'No!' says she, and even as she says it, the door opens and Gladys walks in. She stops on seeing her sisters, and makes an attempt to escape, but Mrs. Croker bars the way.

'Stand and deliver,' says she. 'I've been betraying you to Nan, so you can't get out of it. She won't believe me, so you had better stay here and convince her.'

'To think of a mouse like you marrying a real live lord,' says Nan. 'And such a lord—solemn, severe, learned; "a grave and reverend Seignor!" What courage! I wonder you aren't afraid.'

'He'll slap you,' says Mrs. Croker, who has grown very frivolous since her marriage. 'I can see it in his eye. He thinks you have been badly brought up, and he is taking you to the altar with a view to correcting your vices later on.'

'That's it,' says Nan. 'A high moral sense of duty alone has brought him to the point. He's going to educate you. I've heard of men who do that with their wives. He will send you to school first thing—some school where the use of the birch is well known, and every quarter he will call there, and cross-examine you as to how you are getting on with your lessons. Are you prepared for all this? Better think it over before you finally commit yourself.'

' Pouf !' says the third Miss Delaney with superb disdain, and here I regret to say she does something with her thumb and her nose, that is rather looked down upon as an accomplishment in polite society. ' If it comes to teaching, I fancy I could give him a lesson or two. But he won't do anything of the sort, you'll see. He " calmly " adores me.'

' Does he pretend that? That's his artfulness,' says Nan. ' No, no, you shan't go yet,' as Gladys makes a second ineffectual dive at the door. ' Hold her, Penelope. We have lots to ask you yet. The question is, do you adore him ?'

' Yes, that is it? Do you love him ?' echoes Mrs. Croker.

' Oh, I don't know. Oh, let me go, do,' both sisters are holding her by this time. ' How can I be sure? I never,' giving way to indignant laughter, ' never heard anything so mean in my life. Did I ever bother you as to whether you were in love with George or Freddy ?'

'That's quite another thing. Another pair of shoes altogether—two other pairs of shoes,' says Penelope briskly, to cover Nan's discomfiture. 'George and Freddy are the usual orthodox, everyday, fall-in-love-with-marrying-young-men; but Cashelmore! He's a thing apart! I can't fancy anyone's having the audacity to fall commonly in love with him. His chin—severity itself. His nose a prose poem—a long one too. As for Freddy—— Do you know,' says Mrs. Croker, subsiding into a chair, 'when Freddy did condescend to propose to me, I remember I was always longing to tell everybody how I loved him. One day, when there was no one else handy, except William, and he was always specially nasty about it, I ran downstairs and told Moriarty about it. She was sympathetic, but,' with a lingering touch of respectability, 'I have at times felt a little ashamed of that.'

'So you ought,' says Gladys. 'I'm sure Freddy would have been mad had he known it. Now, if I——'

Confused pause.

'Yes, go on, if Cashelmore were to hear of your

doing such a thing there would be wigs on the green. Just so; the very thing we are trying to impress upon you. A real live lord is a very different thing from an informal commoner. We would have you consider ere it is too late. If you love this man, well and good; if not—— Come, do you love him ?'

' Oh, what a horrid question !' says Gladys, wriggling her pretty slender body in her grasp.

' If you refuse to speak, it will be my unpleasant duty to pinch you,' says Mrs. Hume, fell determination in her eye.

' Oh, don't ! Oh, there ! yes, yes, I do then,' cries Gladys, driven by desperation. ' I love him every bit as well as he loves me. I think there is no one on earth like him. If I found out he didn't love me I should die. There,' indignantly, ' are you satisfied now? Are you ashamed of yourselves? Let me go. Nan, he is waiting for me in the garden. Oh, there he is, just outside the window.'

At this both Mrs. Hume and Mrs. Croker start back guiltily, leaving her free.

' I say, Gladys,' whispers the latter, ' don't tell him what we've been saying.'

'Not likely,' in tones of supreme contempt. 'I shall let him find out for himself the sort of sisters-in-law the poor fellow will have to endure.'

'Well,' says Penelope, regarding her admiringly, it is wonderful. Tell you what,' says Gladys,' giving her a very loving kiss, 'you are a credit to your family.'

'I'll tell you something else,' says Nan, embracing her in turn. 'I have made up my mind to give you a wedding present that will make me a credit to my family—for the first time.'

'Yes, really,' says Penelope, as Gladys makes her escape through the window, 'I suppose it is time to be thinking about that.'

'What? Our credit?'

'No; our wedding presents!'

*　　　*　　　*　　　*　　　*

'Just fancy that little absurd creature marrying into the Peerage,' says Nan that evening, leaning over the back of her husband's chair, and giving his ear a gentle pull, 'whilst Penelope and I, who '— saucily—'are really lovely women, have had to content ourselves with ordinary individuals!'

' Well,' says Hume, laying down his paper, ' what of that ? You know you could not be happier than you are, if you had married a duke.'

' I like that,' says Mrs. Hume, throwing up her pretty head, and then slipping her arms round his neck and giving him a good hug. ' It's true. I couldn't. I'm almost glad, after all, that you did run away with me.'

' Now, Nan—I protest. Are you never to believe the truth about that ? I swear to you I never had the least intention of running away with you.'

' No? Then more shame for you !' says she promptly, with an adorable little laugh.

It is so full of happy life, so sweet, so entirely free from regret of any sort, that Hume, looking at her, feels a sudden wave of gladness move his heart.

' I thank God you are happy—at last,' he says, his tone grave, but full of devout gratitude.

THE END.

LILLING AND SONS, PRINTERS, GUILDFORD.